W9-AVT-259

"Why don't you let me buy you supper?" Theo said. "Your first night in Rome shouldn't be spent by yourself."

"Oh—I don't really think... Wouldn't you rather...? I mean, wouldn't some of your colleagues be more interesting company than me?" Lily began.

"Certainly not," he said lightly. He grinned down at her. "Let me show you some of the places I've been to before, and you can choose which one you like the look of."

His teeth were almost blindingly white as he smiled, and the face, which on first impression had seemed serious and somewhat formidable to Lily, now exhibited a heart-throbbingly purposeful quality, indicating someone strong, reliable...and utterly captivating. The sort of man she might one day paint riding on a white charger to rescue damsels in distress.

Lily choked back her disbelief in her own thoughts. Rome was a mad place! It was making *her* mad!

SUSANNE JAMES has enjoyed creative writing since childhood, completing her first—sadly unpublished—novel by the age of twelve. She has three grown-up children who were, and are, her pride and joy, and who all live happily in Oxfordshire with their families. She was always happy to put the needs of her family before her ambition to write seriously, although along the way some published articles for magazines and newspapers helped to keep the dream alive!

Susanne's big regret is that her beloved husband is no longer here to share the pleasure of her recent success. She now shares her life with Toffee, her young Cavalier King Charles spaniel who decides when it's time to get up (early) and when a walk in the park is overdue!

THE BRITISH BILLIONAIRE'S INNOCENT BRIDE
SUSANNE JAMES

~ INNOCENT WIVES ~

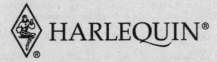

TORONTO • NEW YORK • LONDON
AMSTERDAM • PARIS • SYDNEY • HAMBURG
STOCKHOLM • ATHENS • TOKYO • MILAN • MADRID
PRAGUE • WARSAW • BUDAPEST • AUCKLAND

If you purchased this book without a cover you should be aware that this book is stolen property. It was reported as "unsold and destroyed" to the publisher, and neither the author nor the publisher has received any payment for this "stripped book."

Recycling programs
for this product may
not exist in your area.

ISBN-13: 978-0-373-52748-9

THE BRITISH BILLIONAIRE'S INNOCENT WIFE

First North American Publication 2009.

Copyright © 2009 by Susanne James.

All rights reserved. Except for use in any review, the reproduction or utilization of this work in whole or in part in any form by any electronic, mechanical or other means, now known or hereafter invented, including xerography, photocopying and recording, or in any information storage or retrieval system, is forbidden without the written permission of the publisher, Harlequin Enterprises Limited, 225 Duncan Mill Road, Don Mills, Ontario, Canada M3B 3K9.

This is a work of fiction. Names, characters, places and incidents are either the product of the author's imagination or are used fictitiously, and any resemblance to actual persons, living or dead, business establishments, events or locales is entirely coincidental.

This edition published by arrangement with Harlequin Books S.A.

® and TM are trademarks of the publisher. Trademarks indicated with ® are registered in the United States Patent and Trademark Office, the Canadian Trade Marks Office and in other countries.

www.eHarlequin.com

Printed in U.S.A.

THE BRITISH BILLIONAIRE'S
INNOCENT BRIDE

For all my friends and their lovely dogs who walk with Toffee and me each day in Alice Park

CHAPTER ONE

On a fine July morning Lily got out of the taxi at Heathrow and, after paying the driver, trundled her overnight case towards the entrance.

Her emotions were a strange mix of regret and relief that her contract with Bella and Rosie's family had ended. She'd only been nanny to the eight-year-old twins for a year, but it had been long enough for her to know that she'd made a mistake at trying her hand at this particular occupation. Child-minding was not for her—even though, towards the end, she'd begun to establish a much better relationship with the over-indulged children. Had begun to like them and feel sorry for them—their mother, a single parent, had very little time for them, which was hard on the children. But it was not what she wanted to do with her life. She was honest in admitting that her own background was probably responsible for her sense of inadequacy, and sometimes feeling out of her depth.

Fortunately she'd saved up enough money so that she could afford to be unemployed for a short time while she took stock of her situation. She would easily be able to afford the mortgage on her tiny one-bedroom flat in an unremarkable Berkshire town, and knew that with her cookery diploma she could walk into another job within the hour at any of the countless hotels and restaurants in London if she wanted to. But she was restless, feeling the need for a change but not knowing how to bring it about, so she'd decided to have a couple of days in Rome and visit her brother Sam, who part-owned a small hotel there.

She checked in and was delighted at being upgraded to business class as the flight was overbooked. In the queue waiting to board the aircraft, she glanced at her ticket. She'd booked a seat next to the window—not because she enjoyed watching take-off and landing, but because it seemed to offer a greater chance of not being disturbed on the journey by people who were intent on relaying their life story to anyone who would listen.

As they all waited to board, Lily noted that almost everyone—as usual—was casually dressed, mostly in jeans and holiday wear. For some reason she'd chosen her fine grey suit and a white shirt, together with sheer black tights and high heels, for the journey. Perhaps that was why she had been lucky enough to get bumped up to business class.

At last they all filed on board, and Lily edged her way along the aisle, glancing upwards until she located her seat number. The row was still unoccupied, so she didn't have to ask anyone to get up, and she took her place, glancing idly out of the window at all the activity outside.

After a moment she was suddenly aware of the arrival of the person who would be sitting next to her and, turning her head quickly, found herself gazing up— very far up—into the dark eyes of the most handsome man she'd ever come across in her twenty-six years. He pushed his hand luggage into the overhead compartment and slammed it shut, then sat down and glanced across at her. 'Morning,' he said, non-committally.

Lily coloured up to the roots of her hair, and was conscious of her usual feeling of anxiousness. Her heart was gathering pace rapidly, and the feeling of being trapped was threatening to overwhelm her.

'Oh—hi—' she said, trying to match his lazy attitude and failing miserably. Why should it matter that she was going to be sitting this close to someone like him for a couple of hours? He didn't look the sort who would want to make small talk all the way. His powerfully authoritative manner was obvious at once, and his strong profile and determined chin sent a shiver down her spine. He was formally dressed, in a dark well-cut suit, gleaming shirt and plain blue tie, his black hair was immaculately styled. Why couldn't he have been a portly, elderly, kindly type, instead of this undeniably sexy individual who, Lily was aware, was attracting covetous glances from adjacent females?

He shifted his long legs slightly, trying to make himself more comfortable in the restricted space, then turned to glance at her, noting her stylish appearance, the rather sweet heart-shaped face, the wavy fair hair piled elegantly on top, giving her a brisk, businesslike air. Then he stared past her out of the window, feeling momentarily disturbed inside. And after a second or two, he knew why. It was the first time he had noticed a woman since Elspeth had died.

It had been over a year now—quite long enough for anyone to adjust. But immediately the mental picture of his wife made him think of his three children—his two sons and Freya—who, at nine years old, was so like

Elspeth, with her glossy brown hair and hazel eyes. He frowned slightly as he thought of his daughter. She was the difficult one—the one he didn't seem to have the same rapport with as he had with the boys, he realised. And because of that he'd reluctantly agreed to Freya's request that she should be a weekly boarder at her school, to be with her best friends. He'd been determined to try and keep them all together, a close family, and this move had seemed to dent that somewhat. But he'd finally agreed, and he had to admit that life had become a bit easier without his daughter's occasional difficult temperament to deal with. And the weekends, when the family was complete, were usually trouble-free.

Thankfully, soon they were loaded and ready for take-off, and as the aircraft began bumping rapidly along the runway, Lily caught her breath, her knuckles white as she gripped the arms of her seat.

Feeling her tense, he looked across at her. 'Does this bit bother you?' he asked mildly, and she was surprised at the question, because it indicated a concern for her. Why should a complete stranger care how she felt? About anything? But those few words sent an unexpected rush of warmth through her, and she smiled up at him quickly.

'No, of course not,' she lied. 'I'm fine.'

He raised one eyebrow briefly, clearly not believing her, but said no more, and in a few minutes they were airborne. People began undoing their seat belts, and Lily's companion immediately got up to retrieve his briefcase from the locker above them. Good. He was obviously going to be deep in paperwork. There'd be no need for pointless conversation. He took out a folder, then shut the case firmly—giving Lily a brief glimpse of the name on the identity panel.

'Theodore Montague', she read. That was all, but it fitted the man exactly. He couldn't have been called anything else! But what a handle! Would anyone ever dare shorten it? Did his nearest and dearest call him 'Theo' or 'Ted'? Somehow she doubted it.

Leaning forward, she pulled out a magazine from her holdall, flicking the pages idly She was seldom able to read anything worthwhile on journeys. She couldn't believe how some people could get stuck into a novel, much less concentrate on important matters—as the man next to her was obviously doing…

Presently the chink of cups and spoons announced the arrival of the refreshment trolley, and Lily thought that a cup of coffee would be more than welcome— she'd not eaten any breakfast before she'd left home. A flight attendant came alongside them and gazed down at Theodore Montague, clearly captivated, flickering her false eyelashes at him coquettishly before asking him what he wanted. He turned to Lily.

'What would you like?' he asked, his deeply intense eyes looking straight into her smoky-blue ones, and once again she was touched by his consideration. No one had ever bothered to put her first in these circumstances, she thought.

'Oh—just a black coffee, please,' she replied quickly. 'No sugar…thank you.'

'Snap,' he said easily, and for the first time she saw the uncompromising lips part in a brief smile, giving a glimpse of strong white teeth. He looked up at the attendant. 'Then that's two black coffees, please,' he said casually.

As they sipped the scalding liquid, he looked across at her. 'You don't like in-flight food, either?' he asked.

'Oh, I expect it's quite nice,' Lily replied, 'but in these

cramped conditions, and with everything shrink-wrapped in plastic, I find my appetite disappears straight away.'

'My own thinking exactly,' he said. 'Anyway, on short flights food is hardly an imperative, is it?'

So…they *were* beginning to make conversation— and for once Lily felt totally at ease. With no trouble at all he seemed to have completely disarmed her, and she relaxed in her seat.

'I can't think that either of us are on holiday,' he murmured. His eyes ran the length of her body and back again to meet her gaze. 'We seem to be the only passengers not wearing jeans and T-shirts.'

'Actually, I'm going to visit my brother in Rome for a few days. He part-owns a hotel there,' Lily said. 'And I've got some thinking to do,' she added. Now, why had she said that? she asked herself crossly. It was the sort of thing that would invite him to question her. But he didn't. He gave her a long, slow look, and she had the awful suspicion that he could read her mind and knew all about her already! Which was silly.

'And you—you're not on holiday?' she asked tentatively.

'Grief, no—I've a seminar to attend. I managed to avoid it last year, but I'm due to give a paper this time, so there's no getting out of it I'm afraid. Still…' He smiled that devastating half-smile again. 'I'm sure I'll survive. Rome is a good place to spend a few days—for whatever reason.'

There was a companionable silence between them for a while as the aircraft droned on.

'What's the seminar about?' Lily asked curiously, suddenly wanting to know more about the man, what he did. Would it be marketing? Public relations? Something important in the City? She was surprised at his reply.

'I spend my life thinking about children,' he said casually. 'I lecture in paediatrics, which is all very well, but it means that I don't get to spend much time on the shop floor, so to speak.' He shrugged. 'Still, you can't do everything, and I'm apparently deemed more use on the lecture circuit at the moment.' He paused. 'I expect that will change in due course. Life never stays the same for long, I find.' He pressed his lips together tightly.

Who could ever have imagined the nightmarish situation that had taken his beautiful wife from him so tragically? That an unidentifiable virus would end her life so dramatically, so unexpectedly? It had taught him not to look too far ahead, or to take life for granted.

Lily sensed his change of mood at once, and it made her want to tell him about herself, about things… 'Well, *I'm* hoping to change my life in some way,' she said, 'but I don't really know how to.' She paused. 'I did a cookery course after I left school, which was OK—but I got sick of cooking for other people all the time, even though it was good experience in London hotels and clubs… Last year I thought I'd have a go at nannying…' She shuddered. 'It was not a good move. I think I was unlucky with the family who employed me—very spoiled eight-year-old twin girls. They were awful. But so was I,' she added truthfully. 'They ran rings round me, and I just didn't know how to handle the difficult situations that seemed to crop up on a daily basis. I was beginning to get more switched on by the end of the contract, but not enough for me to contemplate pursuing that particular career any further.' She sighed. 'You have to live in order to learn, don't you?' she said wistfully. 'I'd have loved to love Bella and Rosie, and I did try. But I don't think they wanted to love me.'

He had not taken his eyes from her face as she'd been speaking, and he nodded slowly. 'Everyone hits the buffers at some time in their lives,' he said. 'And all experience—even hurtful experience—teaches us something, I suppose.' He opened the folder on his knees again. 'I do hope you find what you're looking for,' he added quietly.

'It's brilliant to see you again, Lily!'

Lily smiled across the table at her brother, feeling a glow of sisterly affection sweep over her. They were sitting in Agata & Romeo, a bottle-lined restaurant near the main station in Rome, and had just dined on delicious broccoli and pasta in skate soup—one of the many delicacies on the menu. As she spooned up the last mouthful, Lily knew that it certainly wouldn't be the last time she tasted it.

'That—was—divine—' she said, sitting back. 'I was really hungry.'

'Talking of things divine,' Sam said, as he topped up Lily's glass with the rest of the wine. 'Who was the bloke you came off the plane with? Drop-dead gorgeous, or what? He seemed very…attentive as he helped you with your stuff,' he added.

Lily looked away, forcing herself to keep the ever-ready blush from her cheeks.

'Just the man who happened to be sitting in the adjoining seat on the plane,' she said casually.

'Really? There was something…something that suggested a certain familiarity, I thought,' Sam said, looking at Lily curiously. 'I really thought there was something going on there.'

'Don't be silly,' Lily said, picking up the menu to see

what else she'd like. 'I've never met him before. He was just someone…interesting to talk to, that's all.'

Sam said no more—he knew from his short acquaintance with his sister that when she decided a subject was closed, it was closed.

Thinking about it, Lily admitted to being surprised at how short the flight had seemed. She and her neighbor had managed to make light, undemanding conversation for much of the way—during which he'd mentioned that he had three children. He'd also spent some time absorbed in his papers, and she'd been careful not to interrupt him. She'd been genuinely surprised when their approaching landing had been announced.

After a minute, Sam said, 'Is there anything else you'd like, Lily? A cappuccino will do me, but choose away. I want to spoil you.' He paused, thinking how beautiful Lily was. 'I don't get the chance to do that very often, do I?' he went on. 'We really must make an effort to get together more—twice a year is nothing, and now that we've found each other we mustn't waste it.' He leaned across and covered her hand with his briefly. 'Promise that we will manage it somehow, Lily.'

Lily looked back at him, her large eyes warm and moist with almost-tears. Putting down the menu, she turned her palm to hold his fingers tightly. 'You're right, Sam,' she said quietly. 'We must make some dates and stick to them. It's not good enough to let work come first all the time—and, speaking of which, how's the hotel going?' she asked. 'You look very affluent.' She smiled, noting his well-cut trousers and designer open-neck shirt, exhibiting his tanned skin.

'Work's good,' he said. 'A bit too good. That's why

Federico and I don't have time to go chasing girls—or sisters,' he added.

Sitting there with her long-lost brother—two years older than her, attractively open-faced, with his brown hair bleached golden by the Italian sunshine—Lily felt her heart soar, and she felt so ridiculously light-headed she wanted to laugh out loud, to jump up and tell everyone how happy she was. Of course it had to be the wine—or was it simply Rome, with its perfect weather, its magical fountains and warm-hearted people, and the scent of jasmine in the air which had filled her nostrils as they'd wandered along the streets earlier? Or was it because at last she belonged to someone—really belonged to the good-looking man who was holding her hand?

'Do you realise that two years ago neither of us knew of each other's existence?' Sam said. 'All that wasted time when we could have been together,' he added quietly.

Of course Lily realised it. And it was thanks to her seeking out her past—with help from the Salvation Army—that she'd eventually discovered she had a sibling. Their now-deceased mother had borne them both before she herself was seventeen years old.

Lily was honest enough to admit that her ignorance of her early life was probably her own fault... She'd been a rebellious, difficult child, passed from one home to another, one foster family to another—and she'd run away twice. It was no wonder everyone had got confused, including the agencies responsible for her welfare. Her personal details had seemed permanently lost somewhere in the system, and by the time she'd reached sixteen and gone on to train at catering college everyone had been glad to be shot of her. But Lily had an instinctive sense of survival, and had worked hard at the course, and at the jobs she'd subsequently got, finally revelling in the purchase of her tiny flat, her first very own private space, where no one could tell her what to do. At last she was in charge of her own life, her own destiny. And that was how it was going to stay. Always.

Sam, apparently, had been different. He'd told Lily how happy he'd been growing up, behaving himself and always doing as he was told by his foster carers. But he hadn't known, either, that he had any family. When he and Lily had come face to face at last their blood tie had swallowed up those lost years and they'd fallen into each other's arms with hardly any self-consciousness.

'I think a coffee is all I can manage, too, Sam,' Lily said now. 'I don't think I'll be able to eat another thing for the rest of the day.'

'Oh, you'll make room for supper later,' Sam assured her. 'No one eats here until nine or ten o'clock in any case. There'll be plenty of time for you to work up an appetite.'

After lunch they sauntered back along the sun-hot pavements, searching out the cool shade of buildings to walk beneath whenever they could.

'I think I'll pamper myself and have a siesta this afternoon,' Lily said.

'Good idea. And I've some paperwork to go through with Federico, so that'll suit us both,' Sam replied easily.

The small hotel—with a mere four bedrooms—was situated in a narrow lane just off Piazza Navona, and Lily had been allocated a chic room at the front. It was well-appointed and comfortable, and she flopped down on the bed, kicking off her sandals and laying back languidly. She'd changed out of her suit as soon as she'd arrived, and was wondering whether the small amount of clothes she'd brought was going to see her through her three-night stay. She shrugged happily. If she ran out of clothes she'd buy some more! She'd never been an extravagant shopper—she'd never had the money—but, hey, she was on holiday, and she was in Rome! There were no frontiers, nothing to hold back her glorious sense of freedom.

To her amazement, when she woke up Lily realized that she'd been asleep for nearly three hours! She hadn't come here to sleep, she thought. She'd come here to enjoy herself, to explore Rome—as well, of course, as meeting up with her brother.

Sliding off the bed, she went into the bathroom to shower. Although Sam's hotel was air-conditioned, there was a distinct sense of the pervading sultry heat outside, so choosing what to wear would be easy. She'd put on the cream cotton sleeveless sundress with the low neck, she decided. It wouldn't matter if it was still a bit creased—although she'd hung it up as soon as she'd arrived—because who was going to notice her, anyway?

She dressed and brushed out her hair, tying it back in a ponytail. Then she moisturised her face, adding sunblock but no make-up. She knew she was lucky with her complexion which, although fair-skinned, seemed to have an olive under-layer which saved her from burning or freckling. She added just a touch of blusher and lipstick and went downstairs.

There was no sign of her brother, but Federico was on duty, and he came over at once to greet her with the typical approach of the Italian male when meeting a woman. He took her hand and kissed it gently, looking down at her appreciatively with his dusky, bedroom eyes.

'Ah…Lileeeee,' he murmured in his heavily accented English. 'What a charming pleasure to 'ave you to stay here. You are so…beautiful.' He paused. 'You look—wonderful.'

'Thank you, Federico,' Lily said lightly. How could you take these people seriously? she thought. He'd be saying the same to every one of his female guests. Yet she automatically smiled back, responding to his compliments. At least *he* wasn't pretending to be someone he wasn't. What you saw was what you got—a red-blooded Latin male, with no nasty surprises in his temperament and a straightforward, lusty appreciation of the female sex. He made Lily feel feminine, and desirable. And because of his openness, he was totally unthreatening.

Still holding her hand to his lips, Federico said, 'I'm so sorry…Sam is—unwell. He is lying down. Head,' he added, touching his forehead. 'He asks you to see him later tonight.'

'Oh, poor Sam,' Lily said, remembering that her brother was prone to migraines—as she herself was. 'Tell him not to worry, Federico. I'm going off to explore, and I'm quite happy being by myself,' she added, as he went to object. 'Tell Sam I'll see him in the morning.'

People were starting to mill about again in the evening sunshine as Lily wandered around. She'd only been here twice before, but it felt surprisingly familiar as she drank in the atmosphere. She stopped idly from time to time, to watch some artists at work, before buying herself a large vanilla ice-cream. She licked at it appreciatively as she sauntered along. It had to be the most delicious confection known to man, she thought, as the creamy substance coated her tongue and slid down, cooling her throat. The Italians certainly knew how to make the stuff.

Presently she came to the Trevi Fountain, and sat down on a nearby seat to watch the huge gush of water stream from its natural spring. The evening sun shone on the spectacle, lighting up the whole picture like an elaborate stage set, and Lily found herself daydreaming as she sat there, her hands clasped in her lap.

Suddenly a light tap on her arm made her turn quickly.

'Hello, there. What are you doing here all by yourself?'

Theodore Montague was standing there, looking down at her, and Lily felt her throat constrict as she gazed up at him.

'Oh—hello—' she said uncertainly. Well, was it really any surprise that they should meet? she asked herself. Rome wasn't that big a place. She moved over to make room for him to sit down.

He was wearing white trousers and a dark open-neck shirt, his bare feet thrust into strong brown sandals, and Lily felt her heart fluttering anxiously in the usual way. Yet it wasn't exactly anxiety that she was feeling, she thought. It was something else—something she'd never actually felt before—and she wanted to push it away. But somehow she couldn't, so she let the sensation wash over her until, hopefully, it would melt away.

They sat there for several moments without saying anything until he murmured, 'Magical, isn't it?' He turned to look at her briefly. 'Why is moving water so mesmerising?'

'I think that everything here is just magical,' Lily said. 'The weather plays a part, though, of course. Why can't we have some of this in England?'

'It's certainly perfect tonight,' he agreed. 'Though next month might be just a tad too hot.' He paused. 'You could presumably come here to live, if you wanted to?' he suggested. 'Maybe it's the change you're looking for. You said that your brother already lives here, so…'

'No, I have no plans to live abroad,' Lily said at once. 'Perhaps one day I will change my mind, but not yet. I feel that my…fate—whatever it is—lies in England.' She smiled as she looked up at him. 'That doesn't sound very enterprising or ambitious, does it?'

He hesitated for a moment before turning to her properly, holding out his hand. 'Look—this is silly. Why don't we introduce ourselves? I'm Theo Montague—and you know why I'm here…'

'And I'm Lily Patterson,' Lily said quickly, taking his hand briefly. 'And you know why *I'm* here.'

He nodded. 'That's better. I don't care for nameless faces,' he said. 'So…go on telling me about yourself, Lily. You mentioned ambitions. *Are* you ambitious?'

'I think I am,' she said slowly. 'But, as I said before, I don't really know where my ambitions lie. Do I want to go on in catering? Maybe secure an appointment with a wealthy family in a lovely house somewhere in the country, so that I can sit in the garden in the afternoons and paint…?'

'So—you like to paint?'

'Yes, though I don't do it very well—yet. But I'm practising. And I'd love to learn to play the piano. I had some lessons once, when I was a child, but they sort of…stopped…and I never took it up again.'

They'd stopped because at the time, she had been living in one of the homes she'd run away from, she reminded herself.

'I think most children are guilty of that,' he said. 'Starting things and not wanting to go on with them.' He was thinking of Freya as he spoke, who seemed to have lost interest in most things since her mother had died.

There was quite a long silence after that, but Lily realised that she hadn't felt so comfortable, or secure, or so plain contented for a long time. She was painfully aware of Theo's elegant legs stretched out in front of him—the strong, masculine thighs evident beneath the fine cotton of his trousers, the well-kept, unblemished brown toes protruding from his sandals—and she checked herself hurriedly. These thoughts weren't part of her life plan. They weren't part of anything to do with her at all. Suddenly she wanted to go back and see how Sam was feeling.

'I ought to go and see how my brother is,' she said, standing up. 'He crashed out with a migraine after we'd had lunch. He was going to take me somewhere for supper, but...'

As soon as she'd said the words Lily could have kicked herself. She'd fed him the line—and he took it.

'Well—why don't you let me buy you supper instead?' he said. 'Your first night in Rome shouldn't be spent alone.'

'Oh—I don't really think—' Lily began, but he cut in.

'Look, why don't you ring to find out how your brother is—whether he's well enough to take you out? If he isn't, I'm sure he'd be happy to think you were being taken care of. Besides,' Theo added, 'I don't much like eating by myself.'

That would have been the perfect pick-up line, Lily thought, had it been said by anyone other than the man sitting next to her. But she knew it wasn't.

Doing as he said, she rang the hotel from her mobile, to be told by Federico that Sam was still in bed and unlikely to surface before morning. She ended the call and looked at Theo.

'Sam is still out of it, I'm afraid,' she said. 'But wouldn't you rather…? I mean, wouldn't some of your colleagues be more interesting company than me?'

'They certainly would not,' he said lightly. 'We'll have quite enough of each other during the day. The evenings are free, thank goodness, to do what we like with. So—' he grinned down at her '—let me show you some of the places I've been to before, and you can choose which one you like the look of.'

His teeth were almost blindingly white as he smiled, and the face which on first impression had seemed serious and somewhat formidable to Lily now exhibited a heart-throbbingly purposeful expression, indicating someone strong, reliable…and utterly captivating. The sort of man she might one day paint riding on a white charger to rescue damsels in distress.

Lily choked back her disbelief at her own thoughts. Rome was a mad place! It was making *her* mad! That, or she had a bad touch of the sun…

CHAPTER TWO

THEY left the piazza, walking side by side with plenty of space between them as they strolled along. The jostling crowds were an eclectic bunch—families, middle-aged couples wandering hand in hand, and lovers oblivious to anyone but themselves, who stopped at regular intervals to indulge in passionate kissing. At first Lily felt acutely embarrassed when they had to side-step an amorous couple, though it wouldn't have mattered if she'd been on her own, she thought. But witnessing it with Theodore Montague there as well seemed to put a different aspect on everything. He, however, appeared not to notice or care what was going on around them.

He looked down at her. 'I expect your brother has already introduced you to most of the sights, the tourist must-sees?' he enquired.

'Some,' Lily replied. 'But there's plenty I haven't seen—and lots I'd like to visit again.' She stopped to let a small child dash between them as he ran to keep up with his parents. 'Sam never seems to have a great deal of time to spend with me when I visit—he and Federico, his business partner, work so hard, and I understand that he must fit me in when he can.' She looked up and smiled. 'I don't mind. I'm used to sorting myself out alone. It's just lovely to be here with him now and again—to catch up.'

Would they ever manage to catch up? Lily thought. There were so many years to talk about—so many things to explain and discuss. Would one lifetime be enough?

After a few minutes, Theo said, 'It's a bit later than I thought—and I'm getting hungry. Perhaps you'd let me decide where we're going to eat? I promise you won't be disappointed.'

Lily didn't need convincing about that. 'Wherever we go will be fine by me,' she said casually.

'The place I have in mind boasts a panoramic vista of the city—so we'll have two for the price of one,' Theo said. 'Excellent food, and a view as well.'

He was right. And presently, sitting opposite him at a candlelit table, Lily wondered if she was dreaming. This was the stuff of fairy tales, she thought—to be here in this timeless city, on an evening so balmy that there was no need for a shawl to cover her bare neck and shoulders, even if she'd brought one with her that night, and to be sharing delicious food with the handsome Mr Theodore Montague… Not that his appearance made the slightest difference to her, of course, but it was impossible to ignore the glances he attracted from any woman who spotted him. He was after all the quintessential human male that artists and sculptors liked to fashion. He could have been the model for Bernini's *Apollo* himself, Lily thought, smiling briefly at the thought.

While Theo chose swordfish for his meal, Lily selected equally delicious veal wrapped in ham and dressed with sage. For a few minutes they said nothing as they ate.

'You don't drink, then?' he asked, as he refilled Lily's glass with sparkling water, before drinking some of the red wine he'd chosen.

'Not often,' Lily said carefully, privately adding to herself, Not with anyone she didn't really know. And, after all, she *didn't* know him—not in any real sense. Of course it was different drinking with Sam...he was the only man she'd ever been able to feel completely at ease with—and she'd had to wait a long time to experience that, she thought ruefully.

Theo had been watching her covertly as she finished the last of the food on her plate, finding himself really liking his dining companion. The cream dress she was wearing showed off her light suntan to perfection, and her fair hair shone with health. Her eyes were cast down as she ate, and he observed how long her lashes were, unusually dark and moist as they rested on her cheeks. He swallowed, picking up his glass, searching for a word that might describe her—but he couldn't readily find one. She had a sort of diffident air, yet there was an undeniable strength apparent just below the surface. The way she occasionally raised her chin as she spoke indicated a force to be reckoned with at times, he thought. Was she a trustworthy type? Almost certainly. Shy? Not exactly—but not very forthcoming, either. Loyal? From some of the things she'd said her brother obviously meant an enormous amount to her. There was an almost child-like love and regard for him. Theo liked that.

He cleared his throat. 'So—let's talk about your plans for the future,' he said briefly, in a way that he hoped wouldn't appear intrusive. 'In spite of what you've said, I feel sure you've got some good ideas floating around.'

Lily looked across at him, the soft candlelight enhancing the delicate shape of her face. 'No, I haven't—not yet,' she replied honestly. 'I'm waiting for some inspiration—but so far nothing.' She smiled. 'I can't wait for ever, of course,' she admitted. 'My funds will keep me going for a month or two, but not for much longer.' She stopped what she was saying abruptly. This man was a stranger, she reminded herself again. Or nearly. Be careful. Don't get close. Don't let him get close.

She sat back, steeling herself not to become enraptured with the situation she was in—the atmosphere, the company…and the penetrating blackness of those eyes which seemed to enter her very soul. 'Tell me about your children,' she said firmly. 'You said you've got three?'

He paused for a moment before replying. 'Yes. Tom is three, Alexander is five, and Freya is nine.'

'Your wife must have her hands full,' Lily said lightly.

'My wife—Elspeth—is dead,' he said flatly, not looking at her as he spoke, his gaze fixed somewhere over her shoulder into the far distance. 'Fourteen months ago she succumbed to a virus and was gone in three days.' His expression was impassive as he spoke, but those dark windows of his soul said it all, becoming blacker and even more intense as he relived the ordeal.

Lily felt a huge wave of compassion sweep over her. What a shock—what a tragedy for anyone to have to suffer, she thought. She let a moment pass before saying anything. Then, 'I am…so…sorry,' she said quietly.

He shrugged. 'We're surviving it together, the four of us,' he remarked briefly. 'Tom and Alex are just young enough to weather the storm fairly easily—but Freya…' He sighed and looked at Lily, noting that her eyes were swimming with unshed tears. 'Freya has taken it very badly, I'm afraid. There was never any problem with her when Elspeth was alive—she was a bright, easygoing child—but my daughter seems to have a huge, resentful chip on her shoulder all the time now.'

'That's understandable...' Lily murmured.

'Of course,' he replied quickly. 'And, because of that, when she asked I allowed her to be a weekly boarder at her school, to be with her friends. I must say she seems easier now when she's back home—which she is full-time now, naturally, because it's the school holidays. I know she misses her mother, but I can't take her place, and—well...I'm not sure I understand women,' he added, looking thoughtful for a second.

'Are there grandparents around?' Lily asked.

'No—'fraid not. My parents are dead,' he said slowly. 'They were both well into middle age when I came along...' His lip curled. 'I was probably a very unpleasant surprise.' He shrugged. 'They were both practising doctors with busy lives—I never actually saw too much of them during my childhood.'

So, Lily thought, he might have known his parents, but in essence he'd been almost as alone as she had.

'And Elspeth's parents...?' she ventured hesitantly.

'Her father is alive, but he lives in South Africa. We seldom see him.'

'So—who takes care of the children?' Lily asked. 'When you're at work?'

'Well, of course I've had to employ nannies...though they've seldom been asked to stay overnight.' The strong mouth tightened as he spoke. 'As soon as I come home, I'm the one in charge.'

And how, Lily thought.

'But luckily for me I have Beatrice—or Bea—and her husband,' he went on. 'They live nearby. Bea used to help my wife in the house, and then with the babies as they came along. But she's over seventy, and I don't want to take advantage of her good nature, even though she says she loves helping out. Which she's doing while I'm here,' he added. 'She and Joe move in and sleep over until I come back—the kids adore them. But—as I said—I don't want to wear them out.' He leaned back in his chair, crossing his legs. 'It was a good job we hadn't any more offspring, because three are about as many as I can handle… We'd intended having a much larger family, but—well—fate had other ideas,' he said.

'Well—you may yet have more one day…' Lily began.

'Oh, that won't happen,' Theo replied at once. 'I shan't marry again. That's not on the cards.' He paused for a second. 'I have no plans for myself. The children and their welfare, their future—that's all I care about, all that keeps me going.' Who could ever take the place of his beloved Elspeth? Who would he ever *want* to take her place?

Lily shrugged to herself. He was still young, and a very marriageable prospect for any deserving female, she thought. But it was obvious that his mind was made up, and she somehow knew that he wasn't likely to change it.

Thinking that he'd divulged far more of himself than he ever had before to anyone—certainly not to a random female—Theo leaned forward.

'And you?' he asked. 'D'you have any other siblings?'

'No. It's just Sam and me,' Lily replied. 'Though it would have been nice if there'd been more of us.'

'I'm sure you'll make up for that one day,' he said easily. 'Have lots of kids of your own, and—'

'No. I don't want children,' Lily said bluntly. She paused. 'If you'd seen me with those twins…I just don't think I'm a natural mother, that's all. It wouldn't be fair—to any of us.' And I'm never going to be a natural wife, either, she added silently to herself, recoiling at the thought, remembering her past with something approaching revulsion.

'And your parents—they're obviously still alive…?' he went on, making the presumption as Lily could only be in her early twenties.

Lily's spine began to tingle, and she tore her gaze away from his. She didn't want to discuss any more of her life with anyone—certainly not with him. Yet he had been surprisingly honest about his own position, so she found it difficult to be evasive.

'Our parents are no longer living,' she said. Well, who knew where their father was? 'So, you see, we're both orphans, you and I.' She smiled. 'I can't even remember them.'

'Who brought you up?'

'Oh, an assortment of aunties and uncles,' Lily said, looking away. There was no need to say that she'd been a human reject, despaired of by foster carers. Because it hurt her to think it—even to herself.

Theo looked at her for a long moment, sensing an undercurrent of something he couldn't explain passing between them. She was bright, obviously articulate and intelligent—yet there was something about her that reminded him of Freya. She was sad, too, he thought. Not just about being an orphan, as she'd said, but for other, deeper reasons.

The meal ended rather soberly after all that, and, foregoing dessert, they left the restaurant and walked towards St Peter's. Late as it was, there was still plenty of activity everywhere, and Lily realised that she didn't feel at all tired, but relaxed and happy. And she couldn't put that down to the wine, because she hadn't drunk any since lunchtime… It had to be Rome, she thought. With just a little credit going to the man walking along beside her. Theo had been personal, and personable, all evening, but he had not once stepped over that line of familiarity which was unacceptable. She realised that no man had ever made her feel so…protected…so appreciated. He seemed to enjoy being with her, with not a hint of wanting anything more. She breathed in deeply, silently. It was a relief to feel this secure.

Presently Theo said, 'Perhaps it's time I got you back to your hotel.' He looked down at her. 'If your brother has recovered, he's sure to be wondering where you are by now.'

'Oh, he won't be worried about me,' Lily said at once. 'He knows I'm perfectly capable of taking care of myself.' She hesitated, thinking how smug and self-sufficient that must sound. 'It's just that I've had to stand on my own feet for so long I never expect anyone to feel responsible for me in any way,' she explained. 'And—that's the way I like it,' she added.

He nodded slightly. 'Yes—I can understand that,' he said, thinking that he was in much the same position himself. Ever since he'd become a lone parent he'd had to almost fight off the well-intentioned efforts of various women wanting to help shoulder some of the responsibility. But he'd been determined from the outset that that would not happen. This was his problem, and he was going to solve it himself. And he'd done all right so far, he thought—even if Freya was a continual source of worry to him. But he felt sure that it would all come right one day.

'Your brother's hotel is very well situated,' he remarked. 'You said it's off Piazza Navona? Couldn't be better.'

'I know,' Lily said. 'So I don't have to look far for entertainment. The hotel is just far enough away from the beaten track to be surprisingly peaceful. I've never lost a night's sleep there yet.'

It didn't take long to get back, and Theo realised, rather disturbingly, that he didn't want the evening to come to an end. He'd enjoyed himself—really enjoyed himself. Since Elspeth had gone, he'd hated eating alone in foreign countries, and he'd been glad of the chance to invite someone other than a professional colleague to have supper with him. It had been a bit of luck that he'd spotted Lily sitting alone by the fountain, and even more lucky that her brother hadn't been well enough to accompany her. For some reason he felt…lighter—lighter in spirit than he had for fourteen months. But of course the reason for that was quite clear. He'd been on a mission—even if he hadn't been aware of that at first. A project had presented itself, and projects were what kept him going these days. The fact was that he liked Lily— liked the woman's company. She didn't grate on his nerves, which was often the case now, when he was with a member of the opposite sex. And subconsciously a plan had been forming in his mind, without him knowing it. Why else had he quite shamelessly been assessing her all the evening—assessing her character, sizing her up?

Just as they approached the lighted entrance to her hotel, he stopped, forcing Lily to halt her steps. She looked up at him, smiling quickly.

'Well, thank you, thanks a lot for that lovely meal, Theo,' she began.

'No—thank you—for agreeing to come with me tonight,' he said seriously, waiting for the right words, the right moment to continue. 'Actually, Lily, I've been wondering whether you'd…' he began.

Lily presumed that he was going to suggest they meet up again while they were in Rome. But she was here to be with her brother—they only had another two days, after all. She'd have to think of a diplomatic refusal, she thought.

'No—I'm sorry…I really must be entirely free for Sam. We have such a short time here together,' she said, 'and we've not seen each other since last year.'

He smiled down into her upturned face. 'No—no, of course. I wouldn't dream of intruding upon any more of your holiday,' he said. 'It's not that.'

'Oh?' Lily said, immediately feeling foolish and frowning slightly. 'Well…what is it, then?'

Unusually for him, Theo had difficulty finding words, but then he managed to come out with what he had to say in his normal forthright manner.

'Would you… Would you step in and look after the boys for me—just for a few weeks?' he asked. 'I did notice from the address on your luggage earlier that we live in the same town… I'm between nannies at the moment, and I'm in a bit of a fix. I loathe the thought of interviewing yet more girls who seldom turn out as I'd hoped. It would just be for a short time,' he added quickly. 'Not a long-term commitment, but it would give me time to—well, to regroup…while you make up your mind about *your* future. It would be just a tempo-rary thing, I assure you. The children will be back at school in a month or so, so you'd have plenty of time for yourself to make plans, write off for interviews, make telephone calls and stuff… And I pay well over the going rate for the job,' he added, almost afraid to hear her reaction to his request.

Lily sank down on to the low stone wall skirting the entrance of the hotel and looked up at him, amazed at what he'd asked. 'Do you honestly believe that I could be up to the task?' she said. 'I've told you—I don't think I'm any good with children. If you're looking for Mary Poppins, you've come to the wrong person.'

'I'm sure you'd be better than some of the girls I've employed so far,' he said flatly. He hesitated. 'I expect it's my own fault—I must be rubbish at the selection process,' he said. 'They all seem OK at interview—but it never quite works out.' He held her gaze for a moment. 'And— by the way—I'm not asking you to be Mary Poppins. I'm just asking you to be a stand-in until I find her.'

'Well—how many nannies have you employed so far?' Lily asked curiously, still utterly taken aback by the unexpectedness of his proposal. What on earth was she going to say? What on earth did she *want* to say?

'Three in just over a year,' he said. 'I had to sack two of them because they turned out to be totally unsuitable, and the third left because she'd suddenly decided to take off and go backpacking for a year. So then I had to use the temporary services of an agency, and that wasn't ideal at all. The poor kids never knew who was going to be there when they got home.'

Lily swallowed, not sure how to respond. She'd made up her mind that being with children all day was defi- nitely not for her, but deep down she felt that it might not be such a bad idea to fall in with Theo's wishes. It could be a timely stop-gap while she reviewed her future—as he'd suggested.

He broke in on her thoughts. 'If you did agree, Lily,' he said, 'it would mean turning up in time to take Tom and Alex to school in the mornings—though of course they're on holiday for the next six weeks or so—and to pick them up at three. Then giving them their tea and waiting with them until I get back at about seven. I always put them to bed,' he added. 'And of course you'd need to be available all day at the end of the phone to deal with any problems when they're at school. Although I'm obviously contactable in a dire emergency, I cannot leave my post for minor things.' He ran a hand through his hair. 'I suppose what I'm really trying to do—what my subconscious hope is—is to find a replacement for my wife… Which is unreasonable of me, of course. How could that ever happen? How could any staff member fill that sort of gap?'

He sat down next to Lily, the lighting from the hotel throwing strange shadows across his face, and, staring across at him, Lily thought how tired he looked—and a bit lost. She sighed inwardly. Despite all her misgivings, something was dragging her towards accepting his offer. From what he'd said, it shouldn't be too onerous a commission, and his boys weren't likely to be such little horrors as the twins. They wouldn't dare—not with Theodore Montague for a father!

She smiled suddenly. 'Let me sleep on it,' she said. 'I need a little time to make important decisions.'

'Quite right—I'd go along with that,' he said earnestly, sensing victory. Somehow he'd read her mind, and in that brief instant he knew that she was going to say yes to his request. But he also knew that she would make him wait a while for his answer.

The frown on the handsome brow cleared, and he stood up, taking a business card from his pocket.

'My mobile number's on this,' he said briefly, handing it to Lily. 'Give me a ring—any time—with your decision.'

Lily studied the card. 'What if I interrupt something important?' she asked, not looking up at him.

'Oh, don't worry about that,' he said at once. 'Bea also has my number, and she knows she can contact me at any time if necessary. My children come first in my life.'

They eventually said goodnight, and Lily watched for a moment as he strode away to return to his own hotel on the other side of the city. When she went inside, Sam was at the reception desk.

'Oh—Lily!' he exclaimed, coming over to give her a hug. 'I'm terribly sorry about this evening. I'll make up for it tomorrow, I promise. Is everything OK—where have you been?'

'Out to a wonderful supper—and walking about, soaking up the atmosphere,' Lily said happily.

And she *was* happy. She'd had a great evening, and she'd enjoyed a man's company more than she could have believed possible. But most of all bubbling up in her consciousness was the fact that not once had he attempted to touch her, to take her hand or even to brush against her. They had not made physical contact all evening. And that was the best thing of all. No wonder she'd been able to completely relax.

As she got ready for bed, she glanced at the business card again. She'd ring him later on tomorrow, with her acceptance. After all, she'd be daft to turn down the opportunity of marking time—and being paid for it— while she reassessed her future.

CHAPTER THREE

A WEEK later, Lily caught the bus which would take her to the opposite end of the town—the posh end—where Theodore Montague lived. She was too ashamed to drive over in her battered old car, preferring to leave it where it was outside her flat.

It was Saturday, and she'd been invited over to tea to meet the children, and to see where she'd be spending much of the next three months of her life.

Gazing out of the window, Lily remembered again how appreciative Theo had been that she'd fallen in with his request, and he'd accepted the fact that she would give it until the end of October before moving on to pastures new.

'By that time I ought to be able to find someone else,' he'd said. 'Especially if you're around to sit in on the interviews.' He'd paused. 'I do think that a woman is better at assessing another woman in these special circumstances. You'll probably spot the warning signs that seem to have gone over my head so far,' he'd added.

Lily hadn't made any comment, still surprised that he considered her, or her opinion, to be of any value. But it had made her feel good inside—had even made her look forward to the challenge of taking up this unlooked-for post. She would try her best to succeed where others had failed—maybe prove to herself that she wasn't as bad at handling children as she'd thought. After all, it was only going to be for twelve weeks.

The house turned out to be one of a terrace of Georgian dwellings, opening out onto the street, with no front garden. The imposing shiny black front door was flanked on either side by two bay trees, and looked solid enough to keep out the most determined intruder.

Lily took a deep breath as she raised her hand to grasp the large knocker—but before she could make her presence known the door was flung open, and a tall, elderly grey-haired woman stood there, with two small boys jockeying for position in front of her.

'Hello…you must be Lily!' the woman exclaimed. 'Do come in. We've been watching at the window, waiting for you.' She smiled, standing aside for Lily to enter, and almost at once her heart lifted at the genuine welcome she was receiving.

'Yes, I'm Lily,' she said hesitantly. She looked down into the upturned faces of the children, whose interested eyes and ready smiles demonstrated their obvious well-being. 'And you're…Tom? And…Alexander?' she asked.

'No. I'm Alex,' Alexander said promptly. 'I hate people calling me Alexander.'

'And I'm not Thomas. I'm Tom-Tom,' the smaller child lisped.

'I'll remember.' Lily smiled. She turned to the woman. 'And you're…Bea?' she asked shyly.

'That's right, dear—Jill-of-all-trades and mistress of none!' She looked down at the children. 'Aren't you going to say hello to Lily properly, boys?'

'Hi, Lily,' they chorused obediently.

'That's right. Now, Freya is out playing tennis at the moment,' Bea explained, 'but she'll be back in an hour. Do come on through, Lily. Theodore is busy in his private study at the moment, but he'll be finished shortly.'

Lily tried to take in her surroundings all at once—something she was very good at—and she was aware straight away of the luxury which surrounded her. The huge oak-floored entrance hall was enhanced at one end by a massive antique dresser on which stood two golden-shaded lamps, some expensive-looking objets d'art, and in the centre a silver-framed photograph of a beautiful dark-haired young woman. Lily glanced away quickly, not wanting to appear inquisitive—she didn't need telling who that was. It could only be Elspeth, whose picture there—to be met by the gaze of every visitor—told its own story. She was still mistress here. Still the most important woman in the house.

Lily was ushered into a spacious, sunny, high-ceilinged room, with three large patterned sofas facing each other, and various footstools and small occasional tables. There was a mirror over the ornate fireplace, and on the mantelpiece were family photos—the one in the centre being of Elspeth, surrounded by her three children. The full-length windows were curtained to the floor in ivory and red striped material, and although opulence screamed at her from every angle, Lily immediately felt this to be a homely room—a room to be enjoyed rather than admired. To prove the point, the two boys immediately leapt on to one of the sofas and started having a friendly fight.

Lily wandered across to look at the garden, which was not only full of fruit trees and flowering bushes, but also the usual trappings of childhood—a climbing frame and a slide, a sandpit, and several footballs lying in corners.

She looked back at Bea, smiling. 'Everything's lovely,' she said, and the older woman nodded.

'Yes,' she said, 'it is.' She sighed. 'I understand that you've been told of the circumstances here? So sudden…so sad,' she added.

'Yes,' Lily said quickly, glancing across at the boys.

Bea followed her gaze. 'It is beginning to get easier,' she said quietly, 'and we still talk about Mummy, of course.' She raised her voice. 'Now then, boys—who's going to help me in with the tea things?'

The children immediately scrambled off the sofa and followed Bea out of the room, and Lily sank down on to one of the upholstered stools for a moment. She had never set foot in such a place in her life. Bella and Rosie's home didn't even come close, she thought. For a moment, she panicked. What was she doing here? Had she had a sudden rush of blood to the head in agreeing to do this? Theodore Montague might have seemed a pleasant person away from England, but she was in no doubt that he could be very different in a work situation. And that was what she was here for. To work.

She could hear the children's raised voices in the distance—obviously coming from the kitchen—and Lily dropped her head into her hands for a second. Here she was, having to prove herself once more, she thought. Somewhere new, with different people—whose true expectations were unknown.

'Is everything all right?' The well-remembered dark tones cut into her reverie, and Lily raised her head quickly, standing up. Her new employer stood just inside the door, looking across at her with that whimsical expression on his face she'd come to recognise. He was wearing chinos and a dark rugby shirt and his hair was tousled, as if he'd been running his hands through it.

'Of course—yes—everything's fine,' Lily said, not bothering to add that all day yesterday she'd been fighting off a migraine—which would probably account for her light-headedness today, she realised. 'I was just thinking what a beautiful home this is,' she said, smiling briefly.

He nodded, then came over to stand next to her. She seemed even smaller today than he remembered her. Younger, and rather vulnerable… He wondered whether she'd be robust enough to deal with his sometimes obstreperous children. Then he shrugged inwardly. She'd only be here for a few months, and at least once she was back at school his daughter would only be present for two days out of every seven.

'You had no difficulty finding us?' he enquired, glancing down at her. She was dressed in blue jeans and a white T-shirt, her hair tied up in one long plait at the back.

'No, it's an easy address,' she said, in answer to his question. 'And it's actually on my bus route. It only took half an hour.'

'I did offer to fetch you…' he reminded her.

'There was no need for that,' Lily said quickly. 'At least I know what to do if my car refuses to start.'

Just then the tea trolley made its entrance, pushed enthusiastically by Tom and Alex, with Bea coming behind, holding the teapot and hot water.

'Careful, boys,' Theo said. 'We'd like those cakes on the plate rather than on the floor, thank you.'

Everyone sat down, while Bea handed out plates and paper napkins, and Lily glanced around, struck by the easygoing atmosphere. There were dainty little sandwiches, and buttered scones with jam and cream, and some small squares of iced cake. The children, sitting side by side on one of the sofas, tucked in to everything they were offered. Even the three-year-old seemed to have no difficulty in eating food from a plate balanced on his small knees, though he was given a plastic mug to drink his tea from. Lily noticed that there was not a crisp or a sausage or a soft drink in sight—the children were enjoying afternoon tea, and she sensed their mother's hand in that.

Lily automatically glanced up at Elspeth's photograph, captivated by the woman's warm, engaging expression—somehow she felt that she, Lily, was being appraised by someone no longer here, yet whose presence was tangible. *I'll do my best,* she promised. *I will try to do my best.*

Although all the food looked delicious, Lily could only manage one sandwich and a small cake. As usual, when she was on edge, her appetite disappeared. But she was glad of the strong, unsweetened tea, and she allowed Bea to refill her cup. She noticed that Theo was not eating anything at all, but sat beside his sons, a half-drunk cup of tea on the small table beside him.

Conversation was dominated by Bea, telling everyone to help themselves, and the chattering of the boys, who were not in the least shy. Well, they'd become used to countless strangers passing through their lives, Lily thought, so one more was no big deal. In fact, after the first few moments of their initial meeting, she'd been more or less ignored by Tom and Alex. They were beautiful children, with naturally wavy fair hair, but their dark eyes—even at this early stage—exactly matched their father's. Glancing at Theo, she realised that he had been watching her, and she wondered what he was thinking. Well…the fact that she was here at all was his idea, not hers. And it had not been just an idea, either—it had been a plea. A plea she'd found irresistible.

She met his gaze unblinkingly. She'd try to fill this temporary gap to his satisfaction, she thought. They'd all survive her efforts—and it wasn't going to be for long.

When everyone had finished their tea, Theo stood up. 'I think we ought to show Lily the rest of the house, don't you? So that she knows her way around,' he said, and the boys jumped down from the sofa while Bea began clearing things away.

Tom came immediately over to Lily and caught hold of her hand. 'I'll show you,' he said importantly.

'We both will!' Alex said.

'Let's all do it,' Theo placated, tilting a smile down at Lily, and for the next twenty minutes she was given a guided tour.

A beautiful dining room was dominated by a huge mahogany table—obviously used for entertaining, Lily thought instinctively—and there was another smaller, television room with a conservatory attached. There was a study area and, best of all in Lily's opinion, the kitchen, where Bea was putting the tea things away. The room seemed to disappear into the far distance, with cupboards and fitments and cooking facilities at one end, and at the other a long refectory table and benches, with two or three easy chairs alongside. One wall was taken up with shelves that held books and toys, haphazardly placed.

Lily took a deep breath. This wasn't only the engine room of the house, she thought, it was comfortable and homely and where the family obviously liked spending time. It was where she would like to be, too, she decided. Quite apart from the gleaming Aga there was a double oven, and her professional eye had taken in all the details—a marble slab perfect for rolling pastry, huge wooden chopping boards, and what looked like acres of space to put things down. She wasn't going to mind preparing the children's teas here. It was a kitchen to die for.

Upstairs, she was shown Theo's master bedroom, with private study attached. Each of the boys had a room, and there was a spare room as well.

'Freya's room is up on the next floor, where there's another guest room,' Theo said. 'She prefers to be by herself, apparently.' He paused. 'It's the untidy one, I'm afraid. The boys are far better at putting their things away.'

'Thanks for that, Dad,' a voice from behind said suddenly, and they all turned to look at the speaker. Freya had arrived, unnoticed, dressed in tennis whites, and she moved to push past them. She was tall and slight, her long hair hanging untidily around her shoulders.

'Freya—this is Lily, who I've told you about,' Theo said firmly, barring her way. The child stopped just long enough to say, off-handedly, 'Hi—Lily,' before running upstairs to her room.

She hadn't attempted to make eye contact, Lily noticed, but had managed to be just polite enough for her father to do no more than raise his eyebrows helplessly as he glanced at Lily. Lily smiled up at him. Why should the girl show any interest in yet another carer who'd be gone in no time, to be replaced by some other stranger?

'You missed Bea's super tea, Freya,' Theo called up.

'I had tea at the club,' the girl replied.

'I thought you were going to come home for tea today?'

Freya's face appeared over the banisters above them. 'Well, everyone else was staying, so I thought I would as well,' she said.

No more was said, but the dark expression on Theo's face didn't go unnoticed by Lily. Suddenly she remembered something, and, slipping her pretty holdall from her shoulder, she opened it, taking out a large paper bag.

'Are you allowed chocolates and sweets?' she asked the boys, and before she could go on Tom had come to her side to peer at what she was holding.

'Yes—but I don't like chocolate. I only like jellies,' he said.

'Well, what a good thing I brought some, then.' Lily smiled, taking out a packet and handing it over.

'I *love* chocolate!' Alex said, and as Lily gave him a large bar his eyes lit up. 'This is my favourite! How did you know that, Lily?'

'Ah, that's a secret,' Lily said. 'I know a fairy who tells me things sometimes.' She suddenly felt a surge of pleasure run through her. She was being accepted—even if it *was* because of the sweets she'd brought with her.

They all went back downstairs then, and Alex said, 'When are you coming to look after us, Lily? Is it soon?'

'Lily will be here again on Monday morning,' Theo said, answering for her. 'But I'm sure she wants to go home now, because she's probably going out somewhere with her friends tonight. We mustn't keep her to ourselves.'

'Oh, I'm not going anywhere,' Lily said quickly— then wished she hadn't. Didn't every young, single woman go out on Saturday nights? She'd made herself sound pathetic!

'Well, if you're not going out, you can stay and help

Daddy put us to bed,' Alex announced hopefully. 'Can she, Daddy?'

'I'm sure Lily has better things to do…' Theo said. 'Even if she isn't going out.'

'Of course I'll stay—if I can be of any use,' Lily said simply.

The fact was, she already loved being here—enjoyed the atmosphere of this lovely home.

Theo shrugged. 'You've won, then, Alex. Lily can do the honours.' He turned to look down at her. 'Thanks,' he said briefly.

The next hour passed rapidly as Lily took control of a bathing session. There was a lot of splashing, and mucking about with toys, but Lily let them get on with it, not caring too much that she was getting soaked as well.

She spotted their toothbrushes on the shelf, and handed them down to the children. 'Scrub until I've finished counting up to one hundred and twenty,' she said firmly.

Finally, she decided that enough was enough. 'Time's up, boys,' she said, taking one of the big white fluffy towels and holding it up. 'Come on—you first, Tom-Tom.' She lifted him out and held him to her, wrapping the towel around him snugly.

'I can dry *myself*,' Alex said, jumping out as well, and Lily thought what sturdy little bodies they had, and what lucky children they were—to be born into a family like this one—even if their mother *had* died. How could anyone go wrong, literally enveloped in all the luxury and love that was evident here?

They scampered out of the bathroom ahead of her, and once they'd put on their pyjamas were ready to be tucked in for the night. Going into Tom's room, Alex said cheerfully, 'Tom-Tom and me have been sleeping in here together since Mummy went.' He jumped into one of the single beds, and pulled the duvet up around him. 'Because it helps him to go to sleep,' he added. 'And we always have milk to drink before we go to sleep.'

Lily sat down on one of the low chairs beside the bed.

'I have mine cold, and Tom-Tom has his warm,' Alex went on helpfully.

'Well, thank you for telling me that,' Lily said, glancing at the younger child, who was already curled up in his bed, sucking his thumb. She paused. 'Would you like a story before milk or afterwards?'

There was a brief silence. 'We don't usually have stories,' Alex said.

'Ahh—would you like one?'

'Yes, please!' both children chorused.

'Then I'll go and get your drinks, and then you can cuddle down and listen while I tell you a story.'

In the kitchen, Lily had no difficulty locating where everything was, and it took her only a few moments to heat some milk. There was no sign of Theo, and she was glad. She didn't want him standing there, watching her. She'd known almost from the first moment that she was going to get on OK here—as long as she was left to do it her own way, with no one interfering. Alex and Tom were good kids—though she wasn't too sure about Freya, who seemed to have done a disappearing act.

Back upstairs, she gave the boys their milk, then started on the storytelling, deliberately keeping her voice low to encourage them to sleep. She wasn't going to tell them that she couldn't remember ever having had a story told to *her* at bedtime, because what did it matter now? she thought.

It wasn't long before Tom had dropped off to sleep, and Alex was having difficulty keeping his eyes open.

'Tell Daddy to come up and say goodnight,' Alex said sleepily, and Lily nodded.

'Of course I will,' she said. 'And I'll tell you the rest of the story on Monday,' she whispered, getting up. As she turned, she just caught sight of Freya, running up the stairs. Lily called up softly, 'Freya—you haven't had any of the sweets I brought for you.'

The girl turned and stared down. 'I don't usually eat sweets,' she said.

'What—never?'

'Well, only sometimes.'

'There are jellies, and some chocolate—oh, yes—and some mints as well.'

'I do eat mints,' Freya said, coming down the stairs slowly.

'Good. Mints are my favourite, too,' Lily said non-committally. She paused. 'They're in my bag.'

She led the way downstairs, and Freya followed her into the sitting room, where Theo was sitting, reading a newspaper.

He looked up. 'Ah—how did bathing go?' he enquired. 'It sounded fairly dramatic.'

'It was fine,' Lily said, handing the bag of sweets to Freya. 'They're waiting for you to tuck them in.'

He got up straight away, and as he went past Freya ruffled her hair affectionately. 'Did you win your game today?' he asked.

'Naturally,' the child replied, unwrapping a butter mint and putting it into her mouth. 'But we lost the doubles. Gemma and me have worked out a strategy for next time.'

'Sounds ominous,' Theo said casually as he left the room.

It was already gone seven o'clock, and although Lily didn't want to go home, she felt that there wasn't any point in staying any longer. She'd achieved what she'd come for—meeting the children and finding her way around the house—so, standing up, she glanced across at Freya, who'd kicked off her sandals and was stretched languidly out on one of the sofas.

'I'm going home now,' she said briefly.

'D'you have to?' was the unexpected reply, and Lily was genuinely surprised.

'I'll be back on Monday,' she said.

'Yes, but why d'you have to go *now?*' the child persisted. 'It's early.' She paused. 'And I'm hungry.'

Just then Theo came back in, and Freya looked up at him. 'Lily doesn't have to go home yet, does she, Daddy? Could she stay and make my supper? Please?'

Theo glanced down at Lily. 'Perhaps you'd better ask her, Freya.'

'Please, Lily, would you make me some scrambled eggs?' Freya began, and Theo interrupted.

'What's wrong with *my* scrambled eggs?' he said.

'Well—nothing, really, Dad. But I just thought that…'

'Of course I'll stay and make your supper.' Lily smiled. 'And I'll show you how I've learned to scramble eggs so that they don't stick to the pan.'

'In that case, make it scrambled eggs for three,' Theo said easily. 'You'll stay and have some with us, won't you, Lily?'

Lily smiled warmly, ridiculously pleased that she wasn't going home just yet. 'All right,' she said. 'Thanks.'

Freya jumped up. 'Great!' she said. 'And while you're doing it, will you finish that story? I promise not to tell the boys the end.'

CHAPTER FOUR

ON MONDAY morning Lily was up even earlier than usual. She'd never been a late riser, so it was no hardship to be ready for the day by six-thirty. As the children had already broken up from school for the long summer break, Theo had told Lily that there was no need for her to arrive before nine.

After the three of them had eaten the scrambled egg supper at the kitchen table, Theo had insisted on driving Lily home on Saturday night. Bea only lived four doors away, and had been only too happy to sit with the children for the short time it took him to make the journey. Sitting beside him in the sleek, silver Mercedes, Lily had felt like a queen. The soft, cream leather upholstery had given her the impression of being enfolded in pure luxury, and, glancing across at him briefly as they'd moved effortlessly through the traffic, she'd felt almost overwhelmed at being there at all. A chance encounter on an aeroplane had deposited her in the company of this rich, influential man, and it filled her with a pleasurable feeling of security. He was strong, purposeful—perhaps even masterful—she thought, but he'd given no hint of being attracted to her, or whatever it was that usually made her feel so uncomfortable when she was in male company. She breathed in deeply. Live for the now, she had told herself. Don't look forward. Don't look back.

Today she decided that she would drive herself over to Theo's house rather than take the bus—but she wouldn't lower the tone of the neighbourhood by parking right outside! She'd find a space somewhere out of sight, she thought.

Theo came to the door himself in answer to her knock. He was casually dressed, Lily noticed—immediately jumping to the conclusion that he wasn't going anywhere on official business today. Echoing her thoughts, he said, 'I'll be working at home, Lily… I thought it only fair to be on hand—as moral support for you, if nothing else—on your first day.' He smiled, as if guessing what she was thinking, and Lily smiled back, knowing that he was noting every little thing about her.

And why not? Why shouldn't he? She was being given charge of his most precious possessions—his three children—and he would expect high standards in every way. But he needn't bother himself, Lily thought. Despite her fractured background, she was a perfectionist in her own way. She was wearing neatly pressed grey trousers today, and a short-sleeved honey-coloured top that seemed to reflect her freshly shampooed hair, which she'd tied back in a ponytail.

Hearing voices, the boys appeared from nowhere, still in their pyjamas, and Alex said, 'We've been waiting for you. You've been a long time.'

'Have I? I'm sorry,' Lily said, wrinkling her nose briefly. There was an undeniable smell of burning coming from the kitchen.

Theo shrugged mildly. 'Freya is cooking breakfast,' he murmured.

Freya popped her head around the door, her small face flushed. 'Lily—I'm doing you some sausages,' she greeted her, before going back to the stove.

As the boys raced on ahead into the kitchen, Theo explained, 'We're not usually this disorganised in the mornings, but it is holiday time. For them, if not for me. Routine tends to go out of the window, I'm afraid. And the boys wouldn't let me help them get dressed. They insisted that they wanted you to do it.' He paused. 'You seem to be something of a hit already, Lily,' he said casually.

She shook her head. 'They're hoping I've brought some more sweets, no doubt,' she said, smiling.

'Well—come on through,' he said easily. 'Coffee's made.'

The glorious smell of it percolating was even more overpowering than the aroma of charring sausages, and Lily had to admit that, if pressed, she could probably eat something. And certainly enjoy a freshly made coffee.

On the long table, she saw that bowls of cereal had been put out for the children, and the boys immediately sat down and began to eat. Lily was touched to see that they had set a place for her, too. She looked around quickly, wondering where their father usually sat, but he was busy pouring coffee and making drinks for the children, and she realised straight away that he'd either had his breakfast or never bothered with the meal at all.

He came over and filled her cup to the brim. 'Sit down, Lily,' he said. 'Uh…I think the sausages are on their way.' He gave her the merest suggestion of a wink as Freya approached, and the child set the plate down in front of Lily, looking at her expectantly.

'Freya—these look absolutely yummy!' Lily exclaimed. 'But, goodness me—I never eat three at a time!'

'There are more over there,' Freya said, waiting for Lily to start eating. 'D'you like mustard with them, or tomato ketchup? I've put both out for you—see?' She paused. 'Daddy never eats breakfast,' she added offhandedly, 'so I haven't made any for him.'

Lily made a great fuss of enjoying the food, and although the sausages were rather blackened, the centres were cooked well enough, and were surprisingly appetizing. She was able to finish them without any trouble. Though, because Freya was being so sweet, and had cooked them specially for her, she'd have eaten them whatever they tasted like.

Theo drank his coffee and turned to go. 'I'll be upstairs in my study today,' he said briefly, looking down at Lily. 'Bea will be doing the lunches—but please help yourself to anything in the house. The children know how everything ticks—feel free to give me a shout if you need me. And you three,' he said, glancing at the children, 'be *good*.'

Lily smiled, looking up quickly. 'I'm sure we shan't be disturbing you,' she murmured. 'Besides, I know there's a big play park nearby, so we'll probably be going down there later, when everyone's dressed.'

He nodded and left the room, feeling quite pleased with how things were going as he went up the stairs. He'd never seen his children react like this with any of the other women he'd employed. The boys were always quite wary of newcomers, and Freya was always only just on the right side of being rude, her negative attitude permanently on parade. But Lily seemed to have cast a spell on his daughter, who'd got up early to prepare breakfast. And as for cooking sausages—the mind boggled! Long may it last, he thought. And as he went into his study and shut the door he admitted to a very unusual, comforting sensation of…what? Optimism? Or relief? He'd found someone suitable for the kids—even if she wasn't going to be here long. Whatever it was, he knew that he felt slightly less screwed-up about his situation than he had for months. He glanced down at the picture of his wife on the desk, smiling back at her for a second.

Later, Lily and the children trooped down to the park, arriving back in time to sit and enjoy Bea's delicious salad and jacket potato lunch.

'Aren't you having anything, Bea?' Lily asked, looking up at the woman who was busying herself with adding ice cream to the fresh fruit salad she'd prepared.

'No, dear. I'll be going home in a few minutes to have my lunch with Joe… We always eat a bit later than they do here—not that Theo ever has much at all during the day when he's home. I've taken him up a sandwich and a coffee, but once he's shut himself in that study that's usually the last we see of him until suppertime.' She paused. 'He works so hard—he's tireless, really. I worry that he overdoes it, but…' She lowered her voice so that the children, who were chattering loudly, wouldn't hear her, adding, 'We think it's his way of coping with his loss, you know. Burying himself in his work to forget.' She sighed. 'We do our best to lighten the load, but there's only so much anyone *can* do, and Joe doesn't enjoy the best of health now, so we're limited in that way.'

'I know Theo is immensely grateful to you both,' Lily said at once. 'You've been a tower of strength to him…' She paused. 'Bea—what usually happens about the evening meal?' she asked. 'You don't do that as well, do you?'

'Well, holiday times are different—we sort of take it in turns,' Bea replied as she handed out the little dishes of fruit. 'Theo isn't much of a cook, but he can produce simple meals, and I make sure they have a roast or a meat pie now and then as well. We sort of mix and match.' She smiled.

'Well, as long as he doesn't think I'm trying to interfere and take over,' Lily said firmly, 'you can leave supper to me for as long as I'm here.' She looked up at the older woman. 'I'm a trained cook, Bea,' she said, 'so I'm not likely to poison the family.'

Bea looked surprised—and pleased. 'Really, dear? Theo never mentioned that you were a cook—he merely said he'd found someone he knew would be good with the children.' She paused. 'But if you really feel you could do some of the cooking it would be a tremendous help. It's not that I mind at all, you understand, Lily— I enjoy being in the kitchen, especially this one—it's just that I get really tired in the evenings, and by the time I've cleared up I'm pretty exhausted. I know that Theo worries that I'm doing too much,' she added.

'Yes, he mentioned that,' Lily agreed. 'So…I'll square it with him, of course, but from now on leave the suppers to me, Bea. And surely you don't need to come in every single day to do lunches?'

'Well, we'd better discuss all this with Theo and see what he says,' the older woman suggested.

After Freya had been collected to go to her daily tennis session the boys went outside to play in the garden. Lily had a good look in the fridge and freezer.

There was enough food there to feed an army, and if Theo agreed with her suggestion she'd have a great time preparing meals in his fantastic kitchen. She smiled to herself as she thought what a simple task it would be to cater for a family compared with the hectic atmosphere that had prevailed in some of the hotel kitchens she'd worked in, where there had been a constant flow of requests for different dishes. Here she would be her own boss—up to a point—and as soon as she'd discovered the kind of food that the children and their father liked it would be a doddle!

The boys passed the afternoon happily in the garden—especially after Lily agreed to fill their paddling pool for them to splash about in. She was in the kitchen, making a jug of squash to take outside, when Theo appeared.

'How are you surviving your first day here?' he asked, leaning casually against the doorframe and watching as she took down mugs from a shelf. 'Any problems?' He paused. 'Did Freya behave herself this morning?'

'Freya was a model child,' Lily said, 'and happy to push Tom on the swings. She seemed to enjoy mothering him, I thought.'

'Oh, she's fine with the boys,' Theo said slowly. 'It's me who seems to be the problem. When I'm around everything is an issue.'

Lily finished putting the drinks on a tray and glanced up. 'Will you join us for a glass of this? It's so warm today and…you've been shut away for hours.' As soon as she'd said that, Lily shuddered inwardly. What he did was none of her business—and she felt that he was quite capable of telling her so!

But he gave a slightly crooked smile at her words.

'I'm working on a particularly difficult lecture at the moment,' he said, 'and it's giving me some grief.' He shrugged. 'The time simply disappears, I'm afraid. But—yes, thanks, I'll take a glass of that.' He opened the freezer door and took out a tray of ice-cubes, adding them to the jug. 'Perhaps I'll come outside for ten minutes to drink it. Give myself a breather,' he added.

Carrying his glass, he followed Lily out into the garden. The boys immediately dashed up to him.

'We've been making sandcastles—look, Dad,' Alex said.

Theo nodded in the direction the child was pointing. 'Yes,' he said mildly, 'and you've certainly altered the appearance of the lawn, too, Alex. But those castles look good, I must say.'

'They're for me to jump on in a minute,' Tom said, 'when Alex says I can.'

Lily sank down on to a cushioned hammock and handed the boys their drinks, sipping at hers gratefully while Theo perched on the edge of a low, ornamental stone wall. Soon the children resumed their activities.

Lily glanced across at Theo, wondering how best to make her suggestion of taking over in the kitchen. Even though he was apparently watching what the boys were doing, she knew his thoughts were miles away. The handsome face was serious, the black eyes mirroring his thoughts in their intensity, and she cleared her throat nervously. Perhaps this *wasn't* a good moment? But would there ever be one?

'I was wondering…' she began, and he turned quickly to face her, his eyebrows raised. 'It's just that…I was speaking to Bea at lunchtime, and—well…I don't think her husband is too well at the moment—'

'What is it? She didn't say anything to me,' he cut in.

'Nothing specific—I don't think. But she is anxious. So, I…' Lily swallowed. She didn't want to assume anything, or to be officious in any way. 'If you've no objection, I'd be happy to see to all the meals while I'm here,' she said quickly, her words coming out in a rush. 'To save Bea having to come in all the time. Just as a temporary thing, of course,' she added hurriedly. 'I did make the offer to Bea, and she said that as long as you were agreeable she'd be happy to hand over the reins.' There—she'd said it. She hoped he didn't think she expected a raised salary.

'Well, I don't know—' he began, so Lily went on.

'I did explain—when we were in Rome—that I've been trained in cooking.' She paused. 'I can bring over my diploma to show you, if you like…'

He gave a short laugh. 'Don't be an idiot,' he said. 'I don't want to see formal evidence of your achievements. My only doubt is that it might be too much for you. Handling three children is quite enough, heaven alone knows.' He hesitated. 'I don't want to take advantage of you,' he said slowly, 'of your willing nature. I would feel bad asking it of you.'

'But you haven't asked it of me,' Lily said simply. 'I've offered. It's my idea. Anyway,' she went on, 'let's give it a try for a couple of weeks, and see if you all approve of the meals I put in front of you. If you don't, you can sack me and reinstate Bea.'

He grinned down at her. 'That sounds good to me,' he said easily, clearly happy at what Lily had suggested. 'The boys and I are easy enough to please, but Freya can be picky. Or she is at times. Recently she decided to go vegetarian—until she smelt Bea's roasting chicken one Sunday lunchtime, and quickly changed her mind.'

Lily felt relieved that Theo had taken her suggestion on board so easily. 'What time do you eat supper?' she asked.

Theo stood up. 'About six—for the kids, I mean. I have mine after they're in bed—about eight, I suppose.' He looked down at her. 'But feel free to make up some of the rules for yourself, Lily. We're in your hands now. I only hope you don't regret it!'

Much later, after Freya had come back from tennis and the boys had been cleaned up, Lily sat them all down at the kitchen table.

'Now, then,' she said, taking a notebook and pen from her bag, 'I'm going to be the kitchen queen for a couple of weeks, and what I want from you is a list of what you all like to eat—just so that I get it right. Fire away. You first, Tom-Tom.'

For the next half an hour the children argued about everything they wanted put in front of them, and before long it turned into a hilarious game of thinking up horrible suggestions like roasted worms and steamed slugs. But Lily had learned enough to satisfy herself that, as she'd expected, the family ate all the usual dishes—with one or two exceptions.

'Does Daddy like all that as well?' Lily asked, glancing at Freya.

The child shrugged. 'S'pose so. He doesn't have supper with us. We're in bed by the time he has his, so we don't know what he eats.'

Lily frowned slightly at the rather dismissive remarks. Theo was right, she thought. His daughter's attitude was undeniably cool where he was concerned. Lily bit her lip. He was such an obviously devoted parent…the sort any child should be grateful for. She, herself, had never had much reason to be grateful to anyone—but what did children know about gratitude? she asked herself, being honest for a second. Perhaps those bad things in her life, which were so unforgettable, had clouded over and hidden other, happier times which she had chosen to deny.

After Lily had given the children their supper, they all went in to watch television.

'I don't want to watch any of this,' Alex said suddenly. 'Lily—can you tell us the rest of that story you were in the middle of on Saturday?' He came over to her and flopped down on the floor.

Lily was surprised. 'Wouldn't you prefer to see this programme?' she asked. 'You said it was your favourite.'

Tom jumped up and switched off the TV. 'No…come on—let's have the story *instead!*' he shouted cheerfully, at the top of his voice.

Presently, when at last the boys seemed ready for sleep and, worn out, Freya, too, had got herself ready for bed, Lily felt as if she'd lived two days instead of one! The non-stop chatter, the continual questions from the children about everything under the sun—including about her own life—made Lily realise what a challenging job she'd taken on. Yet she'd amazed herself at how much she'd enjoyed the day—at how well she'd coped with it all. Perhaps she wasn't such a hopeless case with children, after all. Anyway, if today was anything to go by, she'd at least manage to live through the rest of her time here. And when school began again, she'd have the opportunity to consider her long-term future.

For now, she'd do her utmost to help Theodore Montague with his offspring—and maybe free up his mind to concentrate on his work. She frowned slightly, remembering the faraway look in his eyes when he'd sat outside with them earlier. He was obviously engaged in something which was giving him food for deep thought… She shrugged. She couldn't help him with any of that, but at least she could take the pressure off him where the family was concerned.

With a sudden rush of warmth she knew, without anyone having to spell it out, that Alex and Tom-Tom and Freya *liked* her. And she *loved* them! From the very first moment she'd felt a distinct kinship with the children—something she hadn't experienced with Bella and Rosie. She couldn't explain it, even to herself, but why bother to try? Enjoy the *now,* enjoy the *now,* she repeated silently. The now would all too soon be the past.

'Can you ask Daddy to come and say goodnight?' Alex said, as he snuggled up in his duvet.

'I was just going to do that,' Lily replied.

She waited a few seconds by the closed door to Theo's room, then tapped gently. 'The children want you to tuck them in,' she said softly.

There was no reply, but in a few moments he emerged, giving her a brief smile. 'I'm finished for today. I'll be down in ten,' he said.

In the kitchen, Lily looked around her thoughtfully. Was she expected to eat with Theo? Or should she just lay a place for him and then make herself scarce? She'd earlier made her own quick-recipe fish pie for the children, and a separate one for their father. It only needed to be heated through, and served with some green vegetables taken from the freezer. Deciding to err on the side of caution, she laid a single place, with a wine glass alongside—she'd noticed an opened bottle of white in the fridge, so Theo probably had some with his evening meal.

She was just putting the steaming vegetables into a dish when he came into the kitchen. He glanced across at the table, then stared down at her for a second.

'Aren't you staying? D'you have to go now?' he asked abruptly, and the way he said it, with his expressive eyebrows lifted just slightly, reminded Lily of the way Alex had looked at her countless times that day.

She hesitated before answering him. 'I wasn't sure whether…' she began uncertainly, and he came right over to stand beside her, his perceptive mind knowing exactly where she was coming from.

'Lily,' he said patiently, 'you are already stepping into a massive breach for me in taking on my children—temporarily, of course—not to mention letting Bea off the hook in here… I want you to consider this your home. In so far as you feel able.' He paused. 'Please have your evening meal with me,' he said. 'I'd like you to…unless you've got other plans?' he added quickly.

Lily smiled up at him, grateful that the point had been cleared up and she knew where she stood. 'I'd be happy to, Theo,' she said. 'I… I did make enough for two,' she added shyly.

Before she could do it, he had set another place at the table, and before she knew it they were sitting opposite each other, enjoying the fish pie.

'This tastes wonderful,' he said. He raised the bottle of wine and glanced at her. 'Will you join me?' he asked. She shook her head.

'I usually only drink water, and I have to drive home, remember?'

He nodded at that, but said no more, remembering

her comment about not drinking alcohol often when they were in Rome. He grimaced inwardly as he remembered one of the nannies he'd employed emptying the gin bottle which she'd discovered in his drinks cabinet. He glanced at Lily covertly as she finished her meal. He liked this woman, he thought. He liked everything about her. He liked her appearance—well, she had a figure that any discerning male would approve of—she was beautiful, well turned-out, and, although she had a reasonably confident manner, there was an underlying vulnerability about her that he found attractive. He was almost thinking *desirable*—but stopped himself just in time. Desire had nothing to do with it—with anything.

They cleared up together, then Theo put coffee on to percolate.

'I really will have to go soon,' Lily said. 'But I'll be back by nine in the morning.'

He smiled without looking at her. 'Go and sit down in the other room,' he said. 'I'll bring this through in a few minutes.'

Now Lily *was* beginning to feel tired—and warm and relaxed after the food, which had proved to be even more delicious than usual. She sat down thankfully on one of the sofas, resting her head back. For a first day it had all gone pretty well, she thought sleepily. There had not been one cross word from the children, and she'd only teasingly had to tell the boys that she was 'counting up to three or else' to get them out of the paddling pool. And Freya—Freya was a sweet child who loved fairy stories. And she had shown such a touching affection for Lily that it made her want to put her arms around the child and hug her. But she wasn't going to do that. Didn't want to get into too close a relationship with any of them. Because it wasn't going to last. By Christmas they'd have forgotten what she looked like.

A call on his mobile had kept Theo in the kitchen for a while, and when he went into the sitting room he saw that Lily was fast asleep, her head drooping gently onto one shoulder, her long eyelashes lying restfully on her cheeks, her hands clasped loosely in her lap. Silently he put the tray down and stood watching her for a few moments. His instinct was to try and make her more comfortable, to put a cushion under her head. But he didn't touch her. Didn't want to disturb her. The poor girl was worn out, he thought. Let her sleep for as long as she wanted to—he'd order a taxi to take her home if it got too late for her to drive herself.

And in the vivid images of early sleep Lily didn't see the children she'd been minding all day. All she saw were the strong, enigmatic features of Theodore Montague as he stared down at her in that rather special way he had. But he was standing at a safe distance away from her, so that it was only his dark, mesmeric eyes that could touch her. Lily shifted just slightly in her sleep, wishing that he would come nearer, just for a second, so that she could lace her fingers with his…

CHAPTER FIVE

By THE time ten days had passed, Lily felt as if she'd been living with the family all her life. She had quickly established a routine that seemed to suit everyone, and was quite glad to be told that a cleaning person came in three times a week to sort out the laundry, dusting and polishing. For everything else, Theo seemed only too pleased to leave it all to Lily. Anyway, by her third day, he was leaving for work as soon as she arrived at nine, was seldom home again before seven—sometimes later. But Lily made sure that there was always a nutritious meal waiting—which she made a point of having with him, as he'd asked her to on that first day.

One evening after supper, as they were clearing up their dishes, Lily said, 'Would it be OK, Theo, for me to drive the children to the moors tomorrow? This lovely weather isn't going to last—so the forecast says—and we'd like to go for a picnic.' She shot him a quick glance, wondering whether he thought she might not be safe behind the wheel—or whether her car was reliable.

'Why not?' he said briefly. 'They'll love that—and there's nothing like eating food in the open air.'

'It's just… I mean…my vehicle is hardly the sort

they're used to being driven in,' she went on, spreading a teatowel to dry in front of the still-warm oven.

He raised an eyebrow, feeling that he knew Lily well enough by now to be reassured that his children were in safe hands, whether in a car or not.

'Oh, that won't matter to them,' he said easily. 'Go and have a great time.' He paused. 'They'll need booster seats, though.'

'Yes. I've got two—which I used when I was looking after Bella and Rosie,' Lily said. 'But I'll need a third one.'

'I'll make sure I take it out of my car in the morning,' he said, following her into the sitting room.

It had become the norm for Lily to stay for a while after supper—just long enough for her to recount the day's happenings. Theo always wanted to hear what had gone on, and she couldn't help observing that Freya was the one most on his mind. He wanted to know how Freya had acted, how Freya had behaved, whether Freya had enjoyed herself. Lily was always quick to defend the little girl, to reassure Theo that the child was perfectly amenable, and in fact was surprisingly mature for her age.

'She loves to help with the boys—and with everything else,' Lily had said, more than once, and Theo had nodded, clearly perplexed at the barrier his daughter seemed to have erected between them.

Now, they sat for a while in silence, and then Theo got up and went across to the window. He turned to glance across at Lily. 'I need to ask another favour, Lily—' he began.

'Ask away. I like doing favours,' she said quickly. She realised, happily, just what a comfortable relationship had developed between herself and her employer. She no longer felt that she had to watch what she said all the time, or to treat him with undue deference. It seemed to her now like a kind of friendship…unhassled and undemanding.

'I have to be away for three nights for a conference. Would you mind staying over?' He paused. 'I would normally ask Bea to step in, but I spoke to her this morning, and she was telling me that Joe is due to have a series of tests this week at the hospital…'

'Of course I'll stay,' Lily said quickly—privately thinking that not going home each night would be much more convenient anyway.' She smiled. 'It's obviously not going to be another trip to Rome?'

'Sadly not. The north of England this time,' he said, looking at her thoughtfully for a moment. The memory of that short stay in Italy had remained with him for a surprisingly long time—and he knew why. This woman was the reason. He still couldn't believe his good luck in finding her. She was the perfect solution to his nanny problem, and she'd come—literally—out of the blue. If he had the guts he'd try and persuade her to stay…to prolong her contract for at least six months or a year. But he knew he couldn't be that selfish. Lily was searching for something far deeper than a job to get by on. She was searching for her future—trying to unwrap some deep-seated ambition, find something that would give her fulfilment. His expression darkened. He liked Lily enough to hope, to *really* hope, that she'd find what she was looking for.

'That's great,' he said, coming back to sit down on the sofa opposite her. 'I leave on Friday and I'll be home Monday.' He leaned his head back and stared up at the ceiling for a second. 'And the other thing which I completely forgot to mention was our holiday plans.' He glanced across at Lily. 'I've booked a couple of weeks at a hotel on the south coast—we've been there before, and it's very child-friendly and supremely comfortable.' He paused. 'I feel it's time you were spoiled for a change—you're spoiling us all the time. I don't want to wear you out!'

She looked across at him blankly. 'You mean…you want me to come as well?' she asked.

'Of course!' he exclaimed. 'I don't know what the children would say if we left you behind. But only if you want to come, Lily. Maybe you'd rather be back home at your place—do your own thing and catch up on your own life for a bit?'

Would she rather be back at *her* place? Not in a million years! She smiled across at him. 'What girl in her right mind would turn down the chance to have a holiday by the seaside?' she said. She bit her lip, already feeling excited at the prospect. 'It'll be a lovely… treat,' she added, not caring if she sounded too willing to fall in with his wishes all the time. The fact was she loved agreeing with everything he wanted. She was living in his beautiful home, looking after his super children—and now she was going to be taken away on holiday for two whole weeks! And being paid to do it! Someone pinch me, she thought. I'm dreaming. I'm dreaming…

The following day, after she'd got the children ready and put the booster seats in the car, they began to put the picnic together. Lily filled some small rolls with ham and cheese, and put Freya in charge of sorting out the orange squash they'd decided to take with them, while the boys were busy choosing crisps and snacks, and putting apples and bananas into one of the baskets.

'Can we take chocolate biscuits as well, Lily?' Alex

of herself well into the background—she'd brought Theo's family here to enjoy themselves, and she was not going to waste time worrying about a headache which she didn't have—yet. Getting up, she called out, 'Shall we play with the ball for a bit before we have lunch?'

There was no reply, and frowning, she looked around her quickly, pulling back some branches to see where the children were hiding. Even though she knew that they were somewhere very close, a tremor of panic ran through her. She'd only taken her eyes off them for a minute or two…

She called out—louder this time. 'Freya—Alex—Tom-Tom…'

Suddenly, from right behind her, they all flung themselves at her so that she almost fell over. Screaming with laughter Freya hugged Lily around the waist.

'We were hiding from you, Lily!' Alex said.

'We made you jump!' Tom-Tom added.

'You *did* make me jump, you little horrors,' she teased, breathing a sigh of relief. What if she'd lost Theo's precious children on their first outing?

Everyone decided that it was too hot to play ball—and also that they were all getting hungry. So they set out the picnic and began eating. Watching them demolish everything put in front of them, Lily thought, Theo was right. There was nothing like enjoying food in the open air. She wondered what he was doing at this precise moment, whether his day was going well, and her mind automatically flicked to thoughts of the supper she'd prepared for that evening. She'd slow-cooked some braising steak in a wine-enriched gravy…all it needed was a crusty lid of pastry on the top and some nice vegetables… The children would have theirs at six, and the rest would be cooked and served for Theo and her to enjoy later. Last night, at home, she'd made a large jar of creamy fudge sauce. She knew the children would enjoy with ice-cream…

When they'd eaten nearly everything they'd brought with them, Alex said, 'What are we going to do now, Lily? Can we go for a walk?'

'After you've had a little rest,' Lily said, starting to put everything back into the baskets. 'I've brought some books for us to look at…'

'Please, Lily—tell us a story,' Freya said, and Lily groaned inwardly. By now she was definitely not feeling good. Her own lunch had consisted of half a roll, a cherry tomato, and almost a full bottle of water. The last thing she needed was to start inventing stories.

'I will later, Freya,' she said.

Tidying everything up, she stacked their belongings into the boot of the car, then sat back down beside the children. Reaching for her holdall, she pulled out her make-up and glanced at her reflection in her mirror—and shuddered. All the tell-tale signs were there… Her face had taken on an ashen shade, and her eyes seemed huge, with dark circles underneath.

As he watched her touch her nose and mouth with a tissue, Alex said suddenly, 'I like your face, Lily. You're pretty.'

Lily couldn't help smiling. That was the last thing she'd have called herself just at this moment!

'Well, thank you for that, Alex,' she said. 'And I like *your* face. I like all your faces.'

They watched her solemnly as she brushed the lightest touch of blusher on to her cheeks in an effort not to look as bad as she was feeling. Glancing at her watch, she saw that it was only two-thirty. They couldn't leave to go home just yet, she thought. She'd have to stick it out for another hour or so.

Somehow Lily managed to keep the children entertained, and to take them for quite a long walk before they all returned to the car, hot and thirsty. By which time the familiar bright zig-zag lights over one eye made Lily realise that she just couldn't go on.

Freya, ever-perceptive, was the first to notice. 'Lily—what's the matter? You look funny.'

The boys stared up at her, and Lily thought that the time for keeping quiet was over.

'I—I shall have to lie down for a bit…I've got a headache coming on, and I can't see very well. I shan't be able to drive us home just yet…'

Just then, her mobile rang, and Lily's heart sank as she took it from her bag. It could only be Theo, ringing to make sure they were all enjoying themselves. But before she could answer it Freya had almost snatched the phone from her.

'Daddy? Lily's got a headache and she can't drive us, and…' There was a pause as Theo spoke to his daughter, and then the child handed the phone to Lily. As soon as she heard his voice, her heart started to race. She couldn't even be trusted to bring his children back home from a picnic—that was what he'd be thinking.

The strong voice made her head ache even more when he spoke. 'Lily—what is it? What's the matter?'

Her reply was faint and feeble as she answered him. 'I'm—terribly sorry, Theo,' she said tremulously. 'I'm afraid I've started a migraine, and I…I forgot to bring my tablets with me…' How pathetic did *that* sound? she asked herself. 'We'll be a bit later home than I thought—I'll have to wait until my vision improves before I risk driving.'

'Stay exactly where you are,' he said at once—and it was a command, not a request. 'Tell me how to find you. I'm coming to fetch you.'

Lily's hand went to her mouth. This was dreadful! He was disgusted with her. That was obvious. Not because she had a headache, but because she was thoughtless enough to forget the all-important tablets. What did that say about her? And why did she care so much, anyway? She cared because she wanted to please Theo, to convince him that she was a suitable person to be in charge of his family—even though her appointment had been his idea and not of her seeking.

Fortunately her mind was clear enough to give him precise instructions as to where they were, and once the call ended she sank back down on the rug they'd left on the grass, the children gathered around her protectively. Even Tom, only three years old, wanted to hold her hand, telling her that she'd be better soon.

Thankful to close her eyes against the mid-afternoon sun, Lily tried to ride out the pulsating throbbing in her temples. She could just imagine how irritated Theo would be feeling—not to say angry. Thanks to her, he'd have to leave his post and rescue them all, probably in the middle of something vitally important at the hospital where he'd told her he'd be working that day.

Lily cringed as she dwelt on it, but must have drifted off in to a kind of semi-doze for a while. It seemed no time before Alex shouted, 'Daddy's here!'

Struggling to sit up, Lily watched him stride along the track towards them, and her mouth dried as he approached. He'd obviously left his car the half-mile away on the road, rather than negotiate the narrow dusty path which Lily had taken.

The children jumped up and scampered towards him, all clamouring to give the news. But he barely looked at them, coming over to Lily and offering a hand to bring her to her feet. She had no idea what he was thinking, because his sunglasses hid any expression, but his voice was kind enough.

'Lily—poor you,' was all he said, and she looked up at him.

'Theo—I'm so…sorry…' she began.

'What for? For getting a migraine?' The question was almost rough.

'No—I mean, I cannot believe that I forgot my tablets. They don't exactly stop a headache, but they delay the worst of it. I should have been able to get us home without having to bother you.' She looked away, feeling unsteady on her feet for a second, and he immediately put a strong hand under her elbow, helping her balance. 'Did I interrupt something terribly important?' she asked.

'No. We'd finished what we had to do—that's why I rang. To say that I'd be home early today.' He looked down at her, conscious that she had leaned into him for support. 'Come on, everyone. Let's get poor Lily home to bed,' he instructed.

Such a huge feeling of thankfulness swept over Lily that she could have cried. He wasn't angry—or if he was he wasn't going to show it in front of the children.

'Everyone help to transfer the picnic stuff to my car,' he said. 'Give me your keys, Lily, and I'll lock yours up for now. I'll arrange for my garage people to come along later and drive it back. It won't come to any harm here for a few hours.'

Overwhelmed now, with thick, steady pain, Lily walked slowly along beside the children, who were all helping Theo carry their belongings towards his car. What an awful end to the day, she thought miserably. And it was all her silly fault that Theo had become involved.

As soon as they got into the house he turned to look down at her. 'Choose your room, Lily,' he said. 'Because you're not going home. You need an early night.' As she looked up to protest, he added quickly, 'Look, you've agreed to stay for a few nights in any case—what does it matter if it's a day early? Tomorrow you can drive back home to fetch your stuff.'

'Is Lily sleeping over?' the boys chorused. 'Yeah! Great!'

And Freya said, 'Please sleep in the room next to mine, Lily! *Please!*'

Theo smiled faintly. 'Do I need to say anything more?' he murmured. 'And don't you dare think about our supper—Freya and I will cope alone, I promise you.'

Lily had got past the point of arguing about anything at all, and she let Freya take her to the guest room she'd be sleeping in. It had an *en suite* bathroom, and was perfectly equipped—apart from night clothes, which didn't matter because as soon as she was alone all Lily had to do was slip off her cotton jeans and shirt and sleep.

Much later—after Theo, with a bit of help from the children, had rustled up cheese omelettes, to be eaten with oven chips taken from the freezer—everyone got ready for bed.

'Can we go in and see Lily?' Alex said, making for the stairs to the second floor.

'No, we cannot,' Theo said firmly. 'No one is to interrupt her or make a noise. She's got to get well enough to look after you three for a few days all by herself, because I shan't be around.'

'That's OK, Dad, we'll manage without you,' Freya said cheerfully, and Theo looked at her sideways.

The remark his daughter had just made hadn't held the normal dismissive tone he'd become used to hearing. It had been more of a reassurance that they would help look after each other, and the hint of a smile tugged at his strong, uncompromising mouth. For a brief second that had sounded just like something Elspeth might have said.

Deep into her drugged sleep, Lily tossed and turned on the pillow, her hair damp with perspiration on her forehead, her dreams vivid and nightmarish. Theo was furious, staring down at her, his anger white-hot as he berated her over and over for her incompetence.

Much, much later, when everyone was asleep and Theo had locked up for the night, he went slowly up the stairs, pausing to look in on the boys before going up to the second floor to check on Freya. He stood for several moments outside the guest room, listening for any sound from Lily. There was complete silence, and he pushed the door open tentatively. She had looked so ill during the afternoon—almost ghost-like. He opened the door wider and stepped inside, going over to the bed and gazing down on her inert form. She was so still lying there, clad only in her bra and panties, her tanned, slender legs slightly bent beneath her, one arm stretched above her head, her hair as pale as a cold winter sky, tumbling around her face. But she was breathing normally.

He took a step backwards, momentarily disturbed at his own emotions. Of course she was an overpoweringly delectable sight—but what was that to him? he thought angrily. She was the young woman he'd engaged to look after his offspring—nothing more, nothing less. He'd only truly desired one woman—had only had one meaningful relationship in his life, with the mother of his children. To whom he'd committed himself for ever. And that was the way it was going to stay. No one could ever, *would* ever, replace Elspeth. Why, then, was his body sending out all these disturbing, persuasive messages, threatening to unbalance his frame of mind?

CHAPTER SIX

WHEN she woke up the following morning, Lily couldn't think where she was. This wasn't *her* room… She'd never set foot in here before! Then memory rushed in and she sat up quickly, recalling everything that had happened yesterday. She cringed again. Theo had been very kind and considerate, she couldn't deny that, but she knew she must have gone down in his estimation. If she was too careless to look after herself, how could she be expected to look after his children?

It was early, and there was no sound in the house. She washed and dressed quickly, before treading lightly down the stairs and passing the children's rooms without going in. If Theo needed to leave soon to go to his conference she'd better get her act together as quickly as possible and check up on a few things, she thought. The smell of percolating coffee drifting up towards her made Lily realise that his day had already begun. She knew that he would have arranged for her car to be brought back here, so she'd drive home now, without delay.

When she went into the kitchen, he had his back towards her as he stood by the stove. Hearing her footsteps, he turned to look down at her.

'Ah—how are you this morning?' he asked, and to her it sounded like the kind of impersonal, polite enquiry he would have made to anyone. He was immaculately dressed in a dark business suit, his black hair gleaming in the sunlight that shafted in through the window, and Lily swallowed, looking away quickly.

'I'm better...thank you,' she replied, matching his coolness of tone. 'I had a very good, long sleep. I'll be fine now,' she added. 'I don't get those attacks very often, so it'll be a while before I get another one.'

'I'm glad to hear it,' he said, and Lily looked at him sharply.

Go on, say it, she thought. Tell me that if I'm going to take to my bed while I'm supposed to be doing my job, we'd better call it a day now. But he didn't say that. He just looked at her closely for a moment.

Even though obviously she was wearing what she had had on the day before, she still managed to look fresh and dainty—and desirable, he thought. With a decisive movement, he turned to pick up the coffee.

'Can I pour you a cup of this?' he asked quietly, feeling annoyed that he was still painfully aware of the sensuous vibes which had troubled him last night. He needed to get away soon—get away from her and concentrate on his work. Work had been his salvation for the last fourteen months, and it would be again.

'No, I'll have tea instead, thank you.' She picked up the kettle and poured some boiling water into a mug, adding a tea bag and swirling it around for a moment.

'Is my car back?' she asked.

'Yes, it is,' Theo said, going over to the table. 'It's outside. When you're ready, perhaps you'd go and fetch what you need from home? I must leave here at eleven.'

'I'll go straight away,' Lily said at once. 'As soon as I've drunk this. There's no sound from the children—they're obviously sleeping in this morning,' she added.

'Yes. They're usually tired after a day in the open air,' he remarked. He had opened his morning paper, spreading it on the table in front of him, and without looking up he said, 'By the way, I think I ought to get in touch with the agency again—about acquiring someone permanent here, I mean. The weeks are going to fly by, and I don't want to be caught out with you expecting to finish up and there being no one to replace you. I'll ring them this morning,' he added. Still not looking up, he said, 'That *is* what you want, isn't it? To be free to change your life?'

'Yes. It is,' Lily said faintly.

Standing by the stove, her mug of tea in her hand, Lily felt as if she'd been punched in the stomach. Her fears had been well-grounded, she thought. After yesterday he couldn't wait to get rid of her—couldn't wait to replace her with a professional. She fought back her tears, sipping at the steaming tea to take control of herself. It was only a couple of days ago that he'd spoken so warmly of the holiday they were all going on together, and she'd felt so wanted, so special…as if she belonged with his family. But today he was different—cruelly different. She hadn't seen Theodore Montague in this kind of mood before. He seemed distant and detached, and for the first time she was being made to feel like the employee that she was. Why had she let herself think that she was liked any more than any of the others had been?

Defiance took over, and saved Lily from letting herself down. She went over to the table and sat down beside him calmly.

'I'll do it,' she said coldly. 'I'll ring this morning, as soon as you've gone. Why don't you leave the number of the agency you like to deal with, and I'll arrange some interviews for the week after next? The week before you go on holiday. Shall I do that?'

'That'll be perfect,' he said obliquely.

Almost immediately Lily drove herself home to collect some clean clothes and other personal belongings. Glancing around at her little flat, she couldn't help comparing it with Theo's place… Chalk and cheese just about summed it up, she thought. Then she straightened her shoulders. It might be a humble dwelling, but it was cosy and private, and always clean and tidy…the way she liked to keep it. She shrugged as she left, locking her front door securely. She'd be back here full-time sooner than she'd thought. Just as soon as a permanent and much more suitable nanny could be found for the Montague family. And that was fine by her!

When she got back the children were up and dressed and running around. Theo stayed just long enough to say goodbye and to tell them all to be good.

'Remember, there are three of you and only one of Lily,' he said. 'So be kind children and do as she asks.'

He turned to Lily for a second. She'd changed into a flowery sundress with a halter neckline which showed off her slender neck and shoulders, and she'd pulled her hair right back in a high ponytail, making her look pure and innocent…and lovely.

His features darkened. He'd better be going, or he'd be late. 'Are you quite sure you're OK today, Lily?' he asked as he went towards the door—knowing full well that she was. There was not a hint of the stress she'd endured yesterday.

'I've told you—I'm quite well, thank you,' Lily replied swiftly, only just managing not to sound as aggressive as she was feeling. 'The children will be perfectly safe with me, I assure you, and I won't drive them anywhere. So please don't worry about them. There's no need.'

He didn't look at her, but shrugged briefly. At that moment he hadn't been thinking about his children, he'd been thinking about her—but she was obviously feeling defensive this morning, guilty because she'd forgotten those wretched tablets, he thought. 'You've got my mobile number,' he said. 'Ring me—any time—if you need to.'

Although there were times when she felt utterly exhausted, the following day passed amazingly quickly for Lily. The children seemed to treat her as a contemporary, rather than someone older, and there was never a shortage of things to do.

On the second day, Bea looked in on them while they were all sitting at the kitchen table doing some colouring.

'Well, well,' she said, leaning over to admire what they were doing. 'What beautiful pictures!'

'We went to the shop this morning, and Lily bought us all new pens,' Alex said, not even bothering to stop what he was doing.

'Yes, and we're making pancakes for tea,' Freya said. 'Lily's going to show us how to toss them.'

'They're going to go right up to the ceiling!' Tom-Tom exclaimed, not wanting to be left out.

Bea smiled down at Lily. 'You've certainly got everything all sussed,' she said kindly. 'I know it's such a relief to Theo that you're here.'

Lily smiled faintly. 'I hope so,' she said slowly. 'But

he's asked me to arrange some interviews…to find someone more permanent to replace me,' she added. As Bea raised her eyebrows, she said quickly, 'And how is your husband, Bea? I'm sorry he's got to have tests.'

The older woman shrugged. 'Oh, well, it happens to all of us from time to time. But he'll be OK, I'm sure. His dad lived to be ninety-nine!'

Bea waited a few more minutes before departing. 'Don't forget to give me a shout if you're desperate, Lily,' she said. 'You know where I live.'

Leaving the children to finish their colouring, Lily went into the sitting room to ring the agency again— and wasn't surprised to learn that there was a shortage of possible candidates at this time of year. There were only two on offer at the moment, she was told, so she made an arrangement for them to come on two consecutive mornings during the week she'd agreed with Theo.

With an undeniably sinking heart, Lily replaced the receiver. Doing this was like sealing her own fate—signing her own death warrant. Yet she knew that was silly. She'd known all along that her contract with Theo was only temporary—her own wish, because she didn't want to be tied down. She'd told him so again the morning he'd left. That she wanted time to make her own plans. But the problem was that she loved her three charges more than she'd ever have thought possible—really loved them. And it was the prospect of saying goodbye to them that was getting to her.

She allowed her thoughts to pause for a moment before continuing with her soul-searching. It was right that she should go, that she should not stay here any longer than necessary, because she admitted to undergoing a sea change in her personality. She admitted to wanting to be near—physically near—to the children's father, and that must never happen. It flew in the face of her determination never to let a man touch her ever again. Up until very recently, the thought had been repellent, disgusting! But, unbelievably, that was beginning to change. And she must not let it. Because she could never again trust a man. Theo was right to take steps for someone else to replace her. For Lily's own sake and sanity she must be prepared to draw a line beneath her present situation and retreat once more into the protective shell she'd formed around herself since childhood.

On Monday there was a call from Theo to say he'd be home later, hopefully in time to see the children before they went to bed. 'I haven't heard from you,' he said to Lily, 'so I assume everything's been OK?'

'We've got on well, thank you,' Lily replied. 'We've had a great time in the park and the garden, and we all went to the local swimming baths yesterday.' She paused. 'They're brilliant swimmers, aren't they? I was impressed—even Tom keeps himself afloat with no difficulty.'

'Yes. My wife took them swimming almost as soon as they were born,' Theo said. 'But I'm quite surprised that Tom agreed to go—he seems to have become rather afraid of it since his mother's not been here.'

'He wasn't afraid at all,' Lily said. 'Of course I stayed close to him all the time—the other two just splashed around by themselves, and Freya can do several lengths without stopping.'

There was a pause, then, 'And you, Lily? They haven't run you off your feet, have they? No more migraines?'

Lily sighed inwardly. He wasn't going to let her forget that in a hurry. 'No,' she said shortly. 'I've been perfectly well, thank you. I told you—I don't expect to get another like that for quite a while.'

He cleared his throat. 'Have you had the torrential rain that we've been enjoying up here?'

Lily was faintly surprised. He didn't seem to want to ring off, she thought. But wasting his time talking about the weather didn't fit the man's persona at all. 'No rain here,' she said. 'Sunshine all the time.'

'Oh, that's good.' Another pause. 'Did—did you contact the agency?'

Lily's throat contracted. Of course! That was what he'd been leading up to. He just hadn't liked to mention it straight away. 'I did,' she replied. 'You'll be seeing two candidates next week—a Mrs Evershot, who's in her fifties, and a Miss Green, who's just qualified. She'd be in her early twenties, I guess.'

'Oh, right. Well, then, we'll have to see what we make of them.' He hesitated. 'I shall rely utterly on your opinion—I don't have much faith in my own where this is concerned.'

Lily swallowed, not trusting herself to speak for a moment. The thought of Freya and Alex and gorgeous little Tom-Tom having to get used to yet another stand-in for their adored mother was as painful to her as it would surely be for them.

Eventually he rang off, and Lily sat where she was, the receiver in her hand. She could still hear his deep, mesmerising, reassuring voice. How was she going to restart her life without them all? she thought, with a feeling of despair touching her.

Theo, standing by the window in his hotel room, was having difficulty understanding himself…having difficulty understanding the rush of tenderness which had swept over him as soon as he'd heard Lily's voice. He breathed in slowly, then exhaled—a long, slow sigh, part-revelation and part-shame that this young woman could reawaken such emotions in him.

Presently, Lily stood up and went out into the garden, where the children were playing. 'Daddy's just been on the phone,' she said, 'and he'll be home at bedtime.' He had not asked to speak to any of them, she noted.

Freya came over to her. 'But you'll be able to finish that next story, though, won't you, Lily? I love it when you leave us halfway through like that, because I try to make up my own ending. I think I know how the fairy is going to sort everything out this time,' she said eagerly.

'Oh, well—if you know, there's no need for me to tell you,' Lily teased.

'Yes, there is!' the child said at once. 'Your endings are always lovely, Lily. The best bit! I just want to know whether this one is the same as mine.'

Lily had to smile. Even the boys liked listening to her fairy stories—she only hoped they realised that that was all they were: stories. She'd hate to be accused of filling their heads with nonsense.

Theo arrived home in time to see the children have their supper—Lily had prepared roasted cod with fresh garden peas, which they'd all helped to pod earlier in the day. When he came into the kitchen, the children jumped down to greet him—though Freya merely held her face up for a perfunctory kiss before moving away. Lily bit her lip. The child showed very little real affection for her father, and Lily knew how deeply hurt he must be.

Much later, when it was bedtime, Theo came too, joining in the bathtime antics as the boys splashed about.

Afterwards he went downstairs, with a request from Lily that he switch on the oven for their own supper. 'I shan't be long,' she told him.

'Lily's got to finish the story before you can have your supper, Daddy,' Freya said.

He grinned, clearly pleased to be back home, and Lily, glancing up at him, thought how young and boyish he looked, his hair damp on his forehead after all the splashing in the bathroom. 'I just hope the story doesn't take too long,' he said over his shoulder, 'because I'm hungry.'

After the children were asleep, and Theo and Lily had eaten their supper, they went into the sitting room with their coffee, each taking their normal places on opposite sofas.

'Have you been comfortable enough here—in your own room, I mean?' Theo said, as he filled their cups from the percolator.

'You don't need to ask,' Lily replied. 'I feel perfectly at home—thank you.' She looked up at him quickly. He'd only asked her to stay for the three nights while he was away—perhaps this was his way of saying that it wasn't necessary for her to stay overnight any longer. But he cut in on her thoughts.

'Well, then, why don't you stay with the arrangement?' he said easily, handing her the jug of cream. 'I can't help thinking that it would be more convenient from your point of view—not having to make the trip across town twice a day.' He drank from his cup. 'It's not that I would expect any more from you—we'd get our own breakfasts—just that for the relatively short time you'll be here with us I should think it would be less irritating, more convenient than having to go home each night.' He paused. 'The children clearly love having you here.'

Now he looked across at her, his searching gaze searing into her. She might have had the total care of his children for the last three days, listening to their endless chatter and cooking for them, but she still managed to look attractive and relaxed, he thought, her complexion clear, her eyes bright as she looked back at him.

Lily, aware of his perceptive scrutiny, was conscious that her colour had risen at his words. Yes, she thought, it would certainly be *very* convenient—for *him!* To have her around twenty-four hours a day would give him complete freedom to come and go as he pleased! But even as she thought that she was ready to give him the benefit of the doubt. He had not taken advantage of her in any way at all since she'd been here, she acknowledged. He was impeccably polite and considerate—especially when they were here alone, she thought gratefully. He was totally unoppressive, leaving her room to breath, and to be herself.

And why shouldn't he be? She was merely his employee, filling an inconvenient gap in his personal affairs.

'Whatever you think best, Theo,' she said coolly, in answer to his suggestion. 'If it suits your purpose then I'll stay. I agree that in some ways it will be more straightforward for me not to have to go home each evening. Though I'll naturally have to return now and again to see to things at the flat…'

'Of course,' he said at once, getting up. 'You can have what time off you like, Lily—so long as you liaise with Bea about covering for the children. That is the arrangement I made with her when you took over—that she'd be on hand if necessary.'

Lily got up then too, and looked up at him. 'Goodnight…I think I'm ready for bed,' she said, and he nodded.

'I'm not surprised.' He hesitated. 'You work hard, Lily—and I— I very much appreciate all you do for us here.'

Well, that was a nice little formal pat on the back for her, Lily thought.

Just then the doorbell rang, and they looked at each other in surprise. It was almost ten o'clock.

'I'm not expecting visitors,' Theo said briefly, moving past Lily and going into the hall. 'And it can't be Bea, because she has her own key.'

He opened the door wide and took a step backward. 'Oliver!' he exclaimed. 'What in heaven's name brings you here? Come in!'

The visitor—tall, fair-haired, and clearly having had a lot to drink—entered the house, clasping Theo's outstretched hand of greeting and looking past him at Lily.

'So sorry to burst in on you uninvited, Theo,' Oliver said thickly. 'I should have rung to warn you, but you know me.'

'Yes, I do, Oliver,' Theo replied cheerfully. 'You were never one for life's little details…but it's great to see you. Come and tell all!' He turned to Lily. 'This disreputable creature is Oliver Crowe, Lily—we've known each other since university. It must be at least three years since we had a get-together.' He paused, turning to Oliver. 'Lily is my children's nanny…'

The man lost no time in advancing towards Lily, towering above her as he took her hand. 'Well, you certainly know how to pick 'em, old man—but then, that is but one of your many gifts, I seem to remember.' He gazed down at Lily, taking in her appearance with a long, salacious stare. Then he turned to Theo. 'I'm in the middle of a mate's stag night—in the town at the

Royal Hotel. There are going to be some antics laid on for later, I believe… I suddenly remembered that this is where you live and thought I'd get a cab and pay you a flying visit.'

He lurched slightly on his feet, and Theo's lip curled slightly. He turned to Lily.

'D'you mind rustling up some coffee for my inebriated friend, Lily? I think we'd better bring him down to earth if he's going to enjoy the rest of the celebrations.'

'Of course,' Lily said, going at once to retrieve their own coffee things from the sitting room, then moving quickly past the men into the kitchen.

As she prepared the drinks she could hear them chatting—Oliver's voice strident and excitable. And as she reached for the cream from the fridge her hands were trembling and colour had risen in her cheeks. Oliver's podgy hand had been clammy in hers, and his fingers had curled suggestively into her palm. His breath, hot and beery, had been overwhelming…she could still smell it. She shuddered, her body trembling right down to her toes.

She stood impatiently by the kettle, which was taking ages to boil. She'd give them their coffee, then disappear rapidly into the sanctuary of her room, she thought.

But before she could do that Oliver had come in to stand beside her, his admiration unrestrained. 'Theo's just gone upstairs to dig out some photos we've been talking about,' he said. He continued staring down at her, and Lily felt herself cringing, her heart doing a mad dance in her chest. 'You're a pretty little thing,' he said, his voice slurring slightly. 'I wonder where Theo found *you*.' He came even closer, nudging his hip against Lily's, and she could feel the soft roll of excess fat around his middle wallow against her thinly clad body.

Suddenly she knew she couldn't stand this a second longer, and wrenched away from him.

'No. *No!*' she cried out. 'Go away—get off!'

With the force of her movement he staggered back, and held on to a chair for support.

'What the…? What did I do?' he said, clearly amazed at her reaction.

Lily was shaking all over, her hands hardly able to continue what she'd been doing. Just then Theo came in. He strode towards her, his dark eyebrows raised.

'What's the matter?' he demanded roughly. He stared down at Lily's flaming cheeks and immediately took the kettle of boiling water from her. 'Here—let me,' he said. 'Did you scald yourself, Lily? When I heard you call out I thought something awful had happened.'

'It's all right…nothing's happened,' Lily said shakily. 'I was just—I was afraid…' She knew she was stuttering incoherently. 'I was afraid that Oliver was going to jog my arm as I was pouring the boiling water. I'm sorry—I'm sorry…'

There was silence for a moment as Theo turned to make the coffee, and Lily was aware that her cheeks were wet with the tears which had formed unstoppably in her eyes. She was aware that Theo had seen them too.

He had realized straight away that something more had gone on, and that whatever it was had upset Lily, who was clearly agitated. Had upset her a lot. And that upset *him*.

He loaded the tray. 'Come on, Oliver. Let's get some of this down you,' he said, in a surprisingly curt tone. He'd known his friend for many years—knew his reputation with women—and although he had only been absent for a couple of minutes it had obviously been long enough for Oliver to try it on with Lily. He glanced down at her. 'You go on to bed, Lily,' he murmured. 'And thanks for doing this.'

The two men left the kitchen and Lily stayed where she was for a few moments, waiting for her heart-rate to lessen, for her breathing to become steady. She knew that tomorrow, when they were alone together, Theo would question her about what had really happened. He would have known straight away that it had been nothing at all to do with boiling water.

And then Lily's tears really did begin to flow, offering her some relief. Because what would be her explanation? How could she tell Theo of the revulsion which had gripped her when she'd felt the heat of his friend's body close in on hers? How could she tell him of the fear which had dogged her nearly all her life…that men spelt danger and disgust and disquiet? Of her conviction that their main function was to control and to seduce until women agreed to their demands?

She took a tissue from the box on the table, dabbing at her eyes. How could she say all that to one of the most handsome, magnetic, mesmerising, totally unmenacing men she had ever met, whose interest in her was solely out of practical necessity? How could she tell him that he was the only man she'd known in all her years she felt she could trust with her very life?

With a shock of realisation Lily knew that, unimaginably, Theo Montague was the first man whose body she longed to feel hard against her own.

CHAPTER SEVEN

To Lily's immense relief, Theo didn't refer to the incident in the kitchen, and the following week passed in the normal way, with him seemingly totally wrapped up in his work. He left very early most mornings, and on three occasions didn't come home for his supper, apparently having evening meetings which ended in a meal somewhere.

When he was at home, although he treated Lily in much the same way as usual, she couldn't help being aware of a slightly different attitude towards her. At the end of each day, alone in her room, she found herself going over and over everything—every word which had passed between them—trying to define the reason for what she saw as his strange coolness towards her. It was not what he said, it was the way she caught him looking at her now and then. And once or twice, when their eyes had met, his gaze had seemed to lock onto hers—which had sent Lily's colour flooding her cheeks, as usual.

Perhaps Oliver had complained to him about her rather irrational behaviour that night? Lily thought. And it might have upset Theo that his friend had felt insulted. Perhaps that was what it was.

But, thankfully, the children were as delightful as ever, and the days passed happily for Lily, making her realise just how much she was going to miss them.

On the Tuesday of the following week Mrs Evershot was due to make an appearance, and although nothing much had been said about it, Lily wondered whether her own presence was still required at the interview. She turned to Theo as she finished clearing their supper things the evening before.

'You haven't forgotten that you're seeing a possible nanny tomorrow?' she asked, not looking at him. 'She'll be here at ten.'

'No, I haven't forgotten,' he said shortly. 'I've made arrangements for someone to cover for me until midday…it shouldn't take too long, should it?'

He looked down at her with that expression in his eyes again, and Lily thought, Why ask me? You've done this sort of thing before—I haven't! But she replied, 'I should think an hour would be plenty… I imagine that one knows almost immediately whether a person is going to be suitable or not…and of course the children's reaction is important too, isn't it?'

He thrust a hand through his hair. 'Yes, of course.' He hesitated. 'It's always tricky,' he added slowly.

'And then Miss Green will be here on Wednesday,' Lily said, trying to lighten the atmosphere by brightening her tone. 'Also at ten o'clock.'

'That'll be OK,' Theo said. 'I've taken that day off, so there's no pressure.' He paused. 'I thought we'd all go out together somewhere afterwards—as a sort of treat.' He stared out of the window moodily. 'This business is hard for them.'

Lily let his words sink in as she stared up at him. *Tell*

me about it, she thought. *I know all about meeting strangers who are going to look after me. I know all about different faces, different personalities, different expectations, different rules.*

'You *will* sit in on the interview with me, won't you, Lily?' he said earnestly, and for the first time since she'd known him Lily detected a sudden lack of his usual self-assurance. This strong, dynamic, highly intellectual man looked a bit lost—bewildered, even—and she dragged her gaze away from him, feeling such an unexpected rush of warmth towards him that she moved right away, out of his orbit, busying herself with rearranging some mugs on the shelf.

'If you think I can be of any practical use, Theo,' she said over her shoulder, 'then of course I'll be happy to meet the women…and give you my opinion. For what it's worth.'

'I'm sure it's worth a lot more than mine,' he replied at once. 'I haven't done too well so far where this matter is concerned—apart from the present incumbent,' he added, smiling. 'You seem to know exactly how to handle my kids, Lily—they've not been this happy, relaxed and contented since—' He broke off before finishing the sentence.

Lily said slowly, 'Maybe that's because I, too, had a succession of different people trying to bring me up,' she said. 'I know how it feels.'

He shrugged. 'Well, whatever the reason, I'm grateful for it. Even Freya seems to have lost that permanently injured expression on her face—except when she looks at me, that is,' he added.

No more was said, and instead of going into the sitting room to have coffee with him, Lily excused herself, saying that she wanted to go to bed, and that she also wanted to make a call to her brother.

Upstairs, Lily went over to the window and stared out across the garden. She felt empty and dispirited—and she knew the reason why. The thought of helping to select another person to have charge of the Montague children was giving her actual physical pain, and she pressed her hands into her sides to try and quell the sensation. She knew the procedure had to be gone through, yet how could she bear it?

Then common sense took over. It had been wrong, all wrong, to let herself get this close to the family, because it was going to end in tears. She knew that the children would hate saying goodbye to her, and when the time came her own heart would be at breaking point, she thought. But her agreement with Theo had only been a very short-term one. She had never seen herself as a full-time carer for other people's children—or any children, for that matter. Definitely none of her own, that was for sure. She shuddered at the thought of the physical obligations which must be endured in creating a new life.

She smiled suddenly as she spotted a tiny field mouse scampering through the grass in the garden. That little creature's plans were far less complicated than her own, Lily thought. All it required was finding enough to eat and to stay alive. Simple, really. She turned away from the window. No, staying here was muddying the waters of her ambition… Surely there was something, somewhere, waiting for her, beckoning to her? Something she hadn't even thought of yet to give her fulfilment? And if she was to discover what it was she needed to break away from this house—and its occupants.

Picking up her mobile, she rang Sam's number. Almost straight away his lovely familiar voice answered.

'Lily! Great to hear you! Tell me all. It's nice and quiet here now, so fire away. How's the job going?'

Lily had told him what she was doing until October.

'The job's fine,' she replied.

There was a chuckle. 'And how's Mr Wonderful?'

'Mr who?'

'Come off it, Lily. We both know who I'm talking about… Mr Drop-Dead Gorgeous who you met on the plane…that *is* who you're working for, isn't it?' Sam persisted.

'Oh, yes, I'm looking after his children,' she said airily. 'But it's work, Sam—work. And it's all coming to an end in no time at all. He's interviewing for my replacement tomorrow, as a matter of fact, and at the end of the summer I shall be footloose and fancy-free once again.' Despite her best endeavours, a stifled sob left Lily's lips as she spoke the words, and she swallowed hard to control herself.

There was a short silence.

'Lily—are you OK? What's the matter?' Sam hesitated. 'He's not giving you grief, is he? Not trying it on…?'

'No, of course not, silly!' Lily blew her nose. 'I was trying not to sneeze just then, that's all,' she lied.

'Well, then, just so long as you take care of yourself, Lily…'

'I'm used to doing that, Sam,' she said. 'I've been doing it all my life, remember?'

'Well, don't forget you're welcome here any time,' he said. 'Come for an extended holiday while you work out your next step—you may even find something here that interests you.'

They chatted on for a while. Sam was still excited about his prosperity, and anxious to share it all with his sister.

Lily smiled briefly as she snapped her phone shut. She still found it hard to believe that she actually had a blood relation who cared about her. Even though they didn't see very much of each other, it was lovely just knowing that he existed. That he was there.

The next morning at breakfast, Theo casually told the children that someone was arriving who might be coming to help look after them. All three looked up at him as he spoke.

'What's she called?' Freya asked flatly.

'Mrs Evershot,' Theo said.

'Is she coming to shoot us, then?' Alex asked.

'I don't like her,' Tom piped up. 'I don't like her name.' He looked across at Lily. 'You won't let her shoot us, will you, Lily?'

Lily had her back to the children while she was making their milk drinks, and she said, without turning around, 'Of course she's not going to shoot you—or anyone else,' she added. 'And anyway, she's only coming for a visit today.'

There was an uncomfortable silence after that, while the children finished their toast, and Theo threw a quick glance at Lily, raising his eyebrows briefly.

She sat down at her place at the table. 'I've organised a very difficult set of tasks for you three today,' she said brightly. She sipped from her mug of tea. 'First of all, you have to search for some of your toys that I've hidden in the garden. There are twelve out there altogether. And then when you've found them you must colour the pictures I've chosen for you to do… If they're good enough, we'll mount them on some sugar paper and hang them up here in the kitchen. And then,' she said, her eyes twinkling across at them, 'there's a very, very, *very* difficult quiz you've got to do.'

'I love quizzes,' Freya said eagerly, drinking in every word that Lily was saying. 'And I'll help Tom-Tom with the answers, because he's only little.'

'That's kind of you, Freya,' Lily said, 'but I've made Tom's a bit easier than yours—and Alex's a bit harder than Tom's. So it's all going to be fair.'

All this information had completely taken over from the thought of Mrs Evershot's arrival, and Theo looked across at Lily as she nibbled at her slice of toast. Her opinion of herself as being rubbish at looking after children was completely unjustified, he thought. She knew exactly how to deal with them—seemed to understand what made them tick, how they were feeling. And she'd obviously spent some time devising the morning's activities in order to take their minds off having to meet another stranger. His expression darkened, and he breathed a long sigh of regret that Lily was going to leave them—that her weeks here were numbered. But he knew that it just had to be... She wanted to spread her wings and fly to some unknown destination, and he would never try to stand in her way.

He knew with painful certainty that it was right she should go...soon. Because he readily admitted to himself that his feelings for her were developing rapidly, with every moment she was around. And that disturbed and even shocked him. The mere thought that anyone should so soon take Elspeth's place in his heart was unacceptable. He had closed his mind to that part of his life—not only because he had made that silent promise to his wife as she died, but also because he would never, ever expect his children to have to try to accept and love a step-mother. Too much had been spoken and written about the enormous emotional difficulties of such a situation—even though there were many happy exceptions to the rule. His children would never have to witness their father loving another woman, sleeping with another woman, speaking in the affectionate terms which had been purely the privilege and right of their mother to another woman. They had suffered enough already.

He shook his head as his thoughts tossed and tumbled in his mind… Why had he ever met Lily? What fateful hand had touched his shoulder and made him ask her to look after his family, to move in with them so that he was forced to be near her, admire her, smell her delightful presence, even seated as she was now, a foot or two away from him? The faint drift of her now familiar perfume tormented him, and he was filled with such a longing to drag her into his arms that he had to stand up quickly, pushing his chair back.

'I'll be up in my study until…for an hour or so,' he said, and Lily nodded.

'As soon as we've cleared up here the children have a lot to do!' She looked down at them. 'I'll give you half an hour to find those toys that I've hidden—and they're not in easy places,' she warned them. 'If something's too easy, it's no fun.'

At precisely ten a.m. Mrs Evershot arrived, and as she opened the door Lily's heart sank. Could this be her replacement? Was this the person who was going to be looking after her charges? The woman was middle-aged, with a straight, no-nonsense kind of face, her grey hair was swept up in a bun at the back of her head, and she was neatly dressed in a suitable grey straight skirt, mid-calf-length, with a matching jacket over a plain blouse.

Lily ushered her into the sitting room, and for the next half an hour or so Lily sat quietly listening to the conversation between Theo and the woman. He was polite and businesslike as he asked her about her previous experience and what she expected if she came to work here. Mrs Evershot didn't leave him in any doubt about that.

'I take it that I shall be living in?' she said flatly. 'But I expect my days to end at eight, after the children are in bed, and to have a day and a half off each week.' She paused. 'I am prepared to organise light meals, but no spectacular cooking. I'm afraid that's not my line. But they won't starve while I'm here.' She flicked at something invisible on her skirt and sat back. 'Also, if I'm required to be with the children during the evenings—say if you have a late function to attend, Mr Montague—then that would be an additional extra to my agreed salary.' She gave him a tight little smile. 'I find it's much better to get all these little details sorted at the outset.'

Lily stared blankly ahead of her, not wanting to catch Theo's eye. This was obviously just a job to Mrs Evershot, she thought. Vocation didn't come into it. She was undoubtedly a supremely efficient woman—but with something other than blood running through her veins. Old memories piled into Lily's consciousness, making her throat dry and her palms clammy. The woman had barely mentioned the children, other than to confirm their names and ages.

Theo stood up—and to Lily's perceptive gaze he looked weary. 'I'm sure you'd like to meet my off-spring,' he said casually. 'They're in the kitchen.'

He brought the children in, and with a painful stab to her heart Lily saw that Freya was holding both the boys' hands protectively. They looked so small and defenceless standing there, with not a smile on their faces. Lily wanted to rush and gather them all to her and run out of the room, run away with them…

After the introductions were made—with Mrs Evershot taking a long, hard look at them all, saying that she was sure they would get on well together once certain rules were established—she stood up decisively.

'Well, there we are, then.' She glanced at her watch. 'I must go—I've two more of these to get through this morning.' She turned to Theo. 'If you consider me suitable, Mr Montague,' she said primly, 'I'll have a tour of the house to see where everything is at that point. The agency informed me that I won't be needed for some time?'

'Yes, that's right,' Theo replied shortly. 'Well into October…'

'Wonderful! That gives me some time to relax before battle commences!' the woman said, with an awkward attempt at jocularity.

As soon as she'd gone, the children flung themselves at Lily.

'I don't like her,' Freya said, without preamble. 'You didn't like her, either, did you, Lily? I could see by your face.'

'And she *is* going to shoot us,' Alex said. 'She said there would be a battle!'

Theo put his arms around his sons, glancing at Freya, who had climbed onto Lily's lap. 'Don't worry,' he said, 'that's the last we'll be seeing of Mrs Evershot.'

Lily eased Freya from her lap and stood up. Theo glanced down at her, a rueful half-smile on his lips.

'Well?' he asked quietly.

'Thanks—but no, thanks, I should think,' Lily said briefly, and suddenly, without stopping to think what he was doing, Theo wrapped his arms around them all—including Lily—in one big circle, so that they formed a close family unit, clutching at each other for support. And being pulled this close to him, feeling his firm muscles tensing against her body, Lily experienced an almost overwhelming need to touch him…to be touched by him.

Just as suddenly he released them all, and walked briskly towards the door to go to his afternoon clinic.

Lily, followed by the children, went into the kitchen to inspect the colouring.

'These are all going to be fantastic!' she exclaimed. 'This afternoon we'll get the paddling pool out, if you like.'

Getting ready for bed that night, Lily could hardly bear the thought of seeing tomorrow's candidate. Trying to be objective about deciding who was to be taking care of the children was almost impossible, she thought. No one would ever be good enough. No one would ever be worthy of the care of Freya and Alex and Tom-Tom. They needed a mother, not a job-seeker—someone who'd be here today and gone tomorrow… They needed consistency and stability—something Lily herself had felt deprived of all the time she was growing up. And while she admitted that she'd often been difficult—had often perversely not *wanted* the latest family to succeed where everyone else had failed—the children living here were blameless. They had done nothing to deserve their present situation.

Sitting late at his desk in his private office at the hospital, Theo stared at the bundle of files in front of him—stared at the computer waiting to receive yet more information about his little patients. All these children had problems—physical problems, some worse than others—which he was doing his best to sort out. He never failed to be thankful that his three were so healthy, only suffering from the normal childish things from time to time. But their pain was a different pain. Their life was not straightforward, either, he thought. Their problem was one which he didn't seem able to relieve. There was no remedy for sadness and acute loss, however hard he tried to think of one.

He'd failed utterly…until he'd met Lily, that was, who seemed to have stepped into the children's hearts as if it had been pre-ordained. If only he could feel, deep inside himself, that it was the right thing to do, he'd beg her to stay with them. For ever. He'd triple her salary—anything to persuade her to have the long-term care of his children until they were old enough to function alone, as young adults. But although she clearly adored them, he was certain she wouldn't agree. Despite her transparently sweet nature, there was a band of steel running through Lily, which he'd detected from the outset, and she wasn't likely to change her mind about anything important—anything she'd set her heart on.

But what about his own needs? he mused, opening the next folder and smoothing the pages down carefully. He knew his children's needs, and he thought he knew Lily's, but what of his own? What about those? He stared blankly at the typewritten information in front of him, only just beginning to accept the undeniable truth that he needed her—not just any woman, but the woman living in his house, nurturing his family. He needed to hold her in his arms, to cover her mouth with his, to actually feel her heart beating in tandem with his own.

This self-revelation made him exultant and despairing at the same time. Exultant because he had admitted, at last, that he was not dead inside after all…and despairing because he knew that this unexpectedly passionate masculine desire would never be satisfied. Not with the woman who seldom left his thoughts.

The following day—ten minutes late for the appointment—Miss Green arrived. She was dressed in a sexy, thigh-skimming multi-coloured sundress, with her long, auburn hair hanging loosely around her bare shoulders, her slender legs tanned, and her feet, with toenails varnished bright red, encased in sparkling strappy sandals.

Lily was faintly amazed at the girl's appearance, which didn't seem quite right for an interview, she thought.

But as if she knew what Lily was thinking, Miss Green said, 'It's such a *super* day—I decided to come in mufti! After all, I'm not on duty yet, am I?' She giggled as she followed Lily into the sitting room.

Theo was already there, and as he'd taken the day off he, too, was dressed casually in light cotton trousers and an open-neck sports shirt. He stood up immediately to greet the visitor, taking her outstretched hand and looking down at her with what Lily saw as typical male admiration. And Miss Green was clearly bowled over by the sight of her prospective employer, who towered above her, his dark eyes glinting, the cut of his jaw pronouncing his total strength and masculinity.

Lily stood well back by the window and watched Theo conduct his second interview.

For the next few minutes she hardly heard a word of

what the two were saying to each other. She was trans-
fixed by Miss Green's uninhibited attitude towards
Theo. Refusing the seat opposite, she sat down next to
him on the sofa, her bare leg resting lightly against his
thigh, looking up at him with a longing expression on
her face, letting her eyes and her long lashes speak
volumes. Theo's richly dark voice resonated domi-
nantly, mingling with the high-pitched little giggle
emerging regularly from Miss Green's fulsome lips. He
stared down, seeming to take in everything about her,
considering her answers to his questions, and as his
elegant head bent slightly to the side, Lily suddenly felt
anonymous—and pointless.

She wasn't needed here at all, she thought. Theo
Montague was quite capable of sizing people up without
any input from her! And sizing her up he certainly was!
He couldn't take his eyes off her! Surely he wasn't
being taken in by the girl's unashamed flirting?

Presently, the boys came in, and Lily noted that this
time they did show slightly more interest than before—
though they still kept their distance.

'Where's Freya?' Theo demanded.

'She says she's not coming down,' Alex said. 'She
doesn't want to meet anyone today.'

Lily moved swiftly. 'I'll fetch her,' she said, and soon
all three children stood waiting to be looked at.

'Oh, aren't they *sweet?*' Miss Green gushed, going
over at once and kneeling down by Tom. 'I love little
boys…*all* little boys,' she added mischievously, looking
up at Theo as she spoke, and then adding as an after-
thought, 'And little girls too, of course!' Then she sat
down again, obviously in no hurry to go.

But Lily couldn't stand being in the room a moment

longer, and went quickly towards the door. 'You must excuse me,' she said briskly. 'I've things to do…'

'Yes, we mustn't keep you any longer, Miss Green,' Theo said smoothly. 'Thank you so much for coming… I'll be in touch with the agency this week.'

Miss Green stood up reluctantly. 'Oh…OK, then…' she said. Barely glancing at Lily, she treated Theo to another of her seductive looks before following him to the door. Finally he closed it, and she was gone.

'Ye gods,' he said, running his hand through his hair. He moved across to stand by Lily, and put both hands on her shoulders. 'Thanks for prising her out of the house,' he said. 'I thought we were never going to get rid of her.'

'We don't like *her,* either,' Freya said cheerfully.

'No, we don't,' Tom said. 'Do we, Alex?'

'Her toes were bleeding,' Alex said. 'There was blood all over her nails.'

As they stood there for a few seconds, Lily let the warmth of Theo's hands seep through her, and when he slid them gently over the tops of her shoulders and down across the length of her arms, it was the nearest thing she had ever experienced to the truly sensual touch of a man— the closest thing to being caressed in the significant way in which a male caressed a female. And she loved it.

Lily felt herself start to tremble. A little bit at first, and then more so. Not with the fear and distaste she knew so well, but with a desire she'd never known she was capable of. And this time she wasn't going to pull herself away and run away and hide. She would stay perfectly still and wish that this moment could be frozen in time for ever.

CHAPTER EIGHT

IN SPITE of having had to meet the two prospective nannies, the children cheered up very quickly—especially as their father was going to be with them for the rest of the day.

'What are we going to do, then, Daddy?' Alex asked, looking up at Theo.

'I thought we'd go to the fair this afternoon,' Theo replied. 'It's only here until the weekend, so we'd better make the most of it.'

'Yes, and Lily is going to sit with *me* in the dodgems,' Freya said. 'You always go with the boys.'

Theo shot her a quick glance. 'If I remember rightly, Freya, last year you refused to go on anything at all.'

'Well…I didn't *feel* like it then, did I?' Freya answered petulantly. 'Anyway, I don't like it when people bang into each other on purpose.'

Lily got them all ready for the trip, letting them choose what they wanted to wear, and presently they came jostling and pushing down the stairs, just as Bea looked in to say hello to everyone. She beamed at the sight of them looking so obviously happy and excited.

'Well—what's on the menu today?' she asked.

'We're all going to the fair!' Alex exclaimed. 'D'you want to come, Bea?'

The woman laughed. 'I've given up on those things, Alex.' She glanced at Lily. 'You're certainly giving them a good time while you're here, Lily,' she said.

'Oh, this was Theo's idea,' Lily said. She paused. 'And it's a good thing that he *is* coming, because I'm not very brave on fast roundabouts and rollercoasters. I shall probably be standing at the side, watching.'

Just then Theo came down, and Bea, looking up at him, was struck by how relaxed he seemed. Her shrewd mind sensed that Lily probably had something to do with that. Her eyes narrowed briefly. It was not right that this highly eligible man should shut himself away emotionally, as he'd undoubtedly done since his wife had died. She and Joe had discussed it privately, many times… Theo was far too young not to have a woman in his life, and, glancing at him now, it seemed to her that the present nanny for his children seemed to be filling several gaps at once.

Bea crouched down for a moment to secure one of Tom's sandals. Wouldn't it be wonderful if Lily could stay on indefinitely? For Theo's sake as well as for the children—who clearly adored the girl. Bea checked her thoughts. She knew she was inclined to be romantic at times—but what if she was? Lily was pretty, intelligent, and so warm-hearted—a man could do worse. And even if her presence did turn out to be the expected temporary arrangement, she might kick-start Theo into realising that permanent mourning was not right. That one day soon he should make a life for himself that wasn't entirely wrapped up in children—his own and other people's.

Bea stood up and pulled Freya towards her, to re-tie her hair ribbon which had come loose. 'Well, now, you all go and enjoy yourselves,' she said, and, giving Theo a sidelong glance she added, 'I think it's time that Lily had a bit of a treat all to herself.' She hesitated. 'Why don't you take her to that special restaurant, Theo—the one you've taken Joe and me to a few times? She'd love it, I'm sure—and with all the cooking she has to do here I think she deserves an evening off, don't you?'

Bea showed not a trace of embarrassment at making the suggestion. She'd been enmeshed in this family's life for so long, in good times and bad, she'd become more like a member of the clan rather than a neighbour of long standing.

Lily coloured up, opening her mouth to protest, but Theo responded at once. 'What a good idea, Bea. Can you do the honours later, then—give the children their supper and put them to bed?'

'You don't need to ask!' Bea's face was wreathed in smiles—her little ploy had worked first time! 'Anyway, I *should* take over now and then,' she said, 'or I shall forget how everything's done.' She turned to Lily. 'What's for supper, Lily?'

'It's cold roast chicken and salad tonight,' Lily said, and Tom broke in.

'Can we have some more of that fudge sauce with our pudding as well?' He looked up at Bea. 'Lily has made fudge sauce again, and it's yummy, yummy, *yummy!*'

'Chicken salad and fudge sauce it is!' Bea said happily. 'I think I can manage that.'

'And before we go to sleep, Bea, can you tell us a story?' Alex asked eagerly. 'Lily does—every night. It's always about a little girl called Eve and a fairy who's her friend, and this fairy makes nice things happen to everyone, and—'

Bea put up her hands in mock horror. 'I'm no good at telling stories,' she said. 'But I'll certainly read to you. Will that do?'

Sitting opposite Theo in the exclusive restaurant, Lily felt all her diffidence melting away. When Bea had put him in such an awkward position earlier, making it impossible for him to disagree with her suggestion, Lily had thought she was going to die of embarrassment. But she had to admit that he'd jumped at the idea. Perhaps he needed to be away from his kids for an hour or two occasionally, for his own sake?

Bea had whispered to Lily that 'smart' was the dress code for the place they were going to, and luckily she'd brought a sleeveless cotton sundress with her when she'd packed to come and live at Theo's home, which flattered her smooth shoulders and suntanned skin. Earlier, Freya had watched Lily get dressed, and gold, rather long and dangly earrings—a present from Sam—had been the child's selection from Lily's modest jewellery case. Lily had to admit that, with her hair coiled up in a simple chignon, the overall effect was good enough.

Freya had sat on the edge of her bed to watch proceedings, and had given her approval.

'You look really, really, *really* pretty,' she'd said. 'I'm going to have a dress like that one day.' She'd paused. 'I wish I was coming with you.'

'Maybe you'll be coming next time,' Lily had said. 'And anyway, Bea is looking forward to being with you… I'm sure she misses you since I've taken over.'

'I think the afternoon was a great success,' Theo said now. 'We've never missed this annual treat yet.'

He stared across at Lily, unable to hide his admiration. She was wearing the dress she'd worn when they were in Rome, and he remembered thinking then how well it suited her. But she seemed to become lovelier every time he looked at her, he thought. Maybe he was wearing the proverbial rose-tinted spectacles where she was concerned, because of the profound effect she was having on his children. They had not been this contented since before Elspeth had died, and that fact alone filled him with a rush of gratitude that he feared he might mistake for something more emotionally significant.

He shrugged inwardly. Stop going on about things, he told himself. He was happy to be here, alone with her, just for an hour or two. His preoccupation at work with children who needed him, and with the constant demands of his own offspring when he was off duty, sometimes made him feel completely submerged—as if he would never function again as a human being in his own right.

Lily smiled across at him, conscious that the flickering candlelight between them made his eyes look mysterious and enticing. She looked away quickly. 'Yes—I think all children like to be terrified of certain things now and then—so long as they're with people they trust,' she said. 'I was surprised how little Tom took it all in his stride, too. He's totally fearless, isn't he?'

Theo nodded. 'Yes—Freya's usually the squeamish one.' He hesitated. 'Although *you* don't seem to be a lover of fairgrounds, Lily. Do the rides upset you?'

'It's not that,' Lily said quickly. 'It's…' How was she going to put this without sounding pathetic? 'It's just that once you're strapped in, and the music starts, and then the ride begins to get faster and faster…well, you can't get off, can you? I always feel trapped. Entirely at the whim of the man working it—until *he* decides when it's all over.'

'You're right, of course. Though that's never crossed my mind,' Theo replied, thinking seriously about what Lily had just told him.

Just then the waiter—a young, attractive man—appeared at their side. 'May I bring you something to drink, Mr Montague?' he asked, throwing an appreciative glance at Lily.

Theo looked across at Lily. 'Will you have some wine this evening, Lily—or would you prefer something else?'

Lily smiled. This didn't seem like an occasion for her usual glass of water. She'd push the boat out! 'I'd love some wine, Theo,' she said. 'But please don't expect me to choose—I don't have much of a clue, I'm afraid.'

He grinned back at her, and Lily's heart gave a small but undeniable leap. His well-cut dark jacket, worn over an open-neck casual shirt, gave the merest glimpse of black body hair, visible against his strong, tanned skin. And his hands as they held the wine list were strong and capable, the fingers long and sensitive.

He pointed out his choice of wine to the waiter, adding a request for some sparkling water, and Lily felt herself relaxing more and more with every moment that passed. As usual, she felt totally unpressurised when she was with Theo, sensing that he understood her, that he could read her mind. And she liked the feeling it gave her.

Leaving them with a copy each of the dinner menu, the waiter departed. Theo leaned back in his chair for a moment.

'You might have declined the opportunity of going on the rollercoasters,' he said, 'but I was impressed at the way you handled that dodgem car. You managed to stop everyone—including the boys and me—from bumping into you. That certainly went down well with Freya—and you seemed to enjoy it, too, Lily.'

'The dodgems are the only things I'll go on,' Lily said, looking down at the selection of food on the list. 'Because I know I can get off if I really want to. Steer to the side and hop out.'

Theo was watching her as she spoke, his analytical mind attempting to penetrate this woman's complex nature. He could see that for some reason she was intrinsically insecure, despite the tangible, feisty undercurrent of strength in her nature.

'Have you ever done that—hopped out of the car while the ride was still going on?' he asked casually, looking down at his own copy of the menu.

'Yes—once,' Lily admitted.

There was silence for a few moments, then, 'You see, I can't bear not to be in control of a situation…' she said simply. 'I have a fear of being…trapped.'

She looked up to see him gazing at her thoughtfully with a look that almost made her melt, and she found herself saying things—unburdening her soul in a way she'd never done before to anyone. 'Do you know, it has taken me a long time to even be able to lock the door in the ladies' loo?' she said matter-of-factly. 'And as for public lifts…' She shuddered. 'But I am improving. I'm not nearly as bad as I used to be. Probably beginning to grow up at last,' she added, somewhat shamefacedly.

He gave a slightly crooked smile as he resumed his examination of the menu. 'Most people have a hang-up about something,' he said. 'The first step is to face it and admit it. Which you've already done.'

Lily chose a lobster-and-prawn terrine to start her meal, followed by braised calves' liver, and she looked across at Theo gratefully. 'It really will be nice to have dinner cooked for me,' she said. 'Thanks for bringing me, Theo.'

'Not at all. Bea was quite right—as she always is,' he said easily. 'It's high time that you sat back and were served for a change. I should have thought of it myself.' He paused. 'To tell the truth, you seem to understand exactly what we all like to eat, so it's very tempting to stay at home and enjoy it—especially as the average place I eat when I'm away isn't a patch on what you do.'

Lily couldn't help feeling gratified by his remarks— and she knew that he meant every word he said. Theodore Montague never used unnecessary pleasantries, whatever he was talking about.

The wine arrived, followed almost immediately by the food. Theo had decided to have the same as Lily and they ate in companionable silence for a while. It wasn't until they'd almost finished the bottle of wine, and were waiting for their desserts to arrive, that Theo said casually, 'Tell me all about yourself, Lily.' He paused. 'I know quite a lot already, of course—not only from what you've told me, but from what the children say about you. But…for example…where were you born?'

Lily looked down, twisting the corner of her crumpled napkin before considering her answer. She never discussed her past with anyone—not that many had ever bothered to enquire in any case. In her opinion, her past was so inglorious it was better hidden.

'I was born in Hampshire,' she said shortly. 'But we…we moved about the country quite a bit—never in one place for long. Our parents died when Sam and I were very young.' She bit her lip. She was trying to tell the truth without giving away too much.

'Yes, I remember you telling me that you were brought up by other family members,' Theo said, twirling the stem of his wine glass slowly. 'Do you see any of them now?'

'No. I'm afraid we've all lost touch,' Lily muttered, conscious that her tongue was beginning to dry at all this questioning. 'Sam and I are the only ones in close touch now.'

How awful did that make her sound? she thought. He'd be bound to think her very ungrateful to abandon the relatives who'd looked after her.

Theo emptied the last of the wine into their glasses and looked at her steadily. His next question hit Lily like a bolt from the blue.

'Have you ever been married, Lily?' he asked bluntly.

Her reply was just as blunt. 'No. I have not,' she said shortly, picking up her glass and taking a large gulp. 'I don't want to be married. I don't want to be tied down in any way. Ever.'

He raised one eyebrow, but let the matter drop, and soon the subject of the two interviewees arose.

'I thought both those women were appalling, didn't you?' he asked casually.

'Yes, I did.' Lily paused. 'I think we should try another agency. There must be more suitable people around than them.'

He waited a moment before answering. 'Yes. That's a good idea,' he said slowly. 'But it'll have to wait until after the holiday now—there's no time left this week, is there?'

His mood had changed in an instant, and, sensing it, Lily wanted to cry out, Don't employ anyone else…the children have had enough to put up with already. But how could she say that when she couldn't offer a suitable alternative? She'd told him enough times that she was seeking pastures new...but what he *didn't* know, and never could, was that—incredibly—she had discovered what being 'in love' was... Had allowed herself to fall for a man who had told her from the start that his children were the only thing that mattered to him and that that would never change.

They, the children, had become just as important to her, too, she thought. But if she *were* to extend the agreement she had with Theo for longer—say for a year or two—how could she stay on and be close to him without one day betraying her feelings? And what if he ever found out about her background? So different from his own privileged one? How could she ever bring herself to tell him that she had lived so much of her life on the human scrapheap, passed from pillar to post? The situation was quite useless, she thought miserably. Staying on here with this family that she'd come to really love could never work out.

Lily was a realist. She knew she must accept her time with them as being one of life's experiences and learn from it. And move on.

Tearing herself away from all this introspection, she said steadily, 'Yes, we might as well put the nanny subject on the back burner until after the holiday.' She was realising that being away with the family—with him—for two whole weeks wasn't going to help, either. It would just make things worse for her emotional turmoil—make her even more aware of what she was having to give up and forget.

With that minor decision made, Theo seemed to cheer up again. 'I've booked the family suite for the children and me,' he said. 'The one we've had before. Luckily the hotel had a vacant room for you next door to us. Though I can't promise that you won't have one or two—or three—small intruders from time to time during our stay…'

'The children are always welcome—wherever I am,' Lily said coolly.

Theo looked at her sharply. She suddenly looked very tired, he thought. He hoped the wine hadn't gone to her head—he knew that she rarely drank. She had been so relaxed and chatty earlier, but now there was a distinct change, a wistfulness about her.

It was almost eleven o'clock when they left the restaurant, and Lily turned to look at Theo as they drove rapidly through the lessening traffic. They had not said much to each other for the last few minutes, and she thought that he was probably glad that the evening was over. He'd done his duty, given her a little treat, and now he was anxious to get back.

'Thank you very much for this evening. It was lovely food,' she said formally.

'My pleasure,' he said, without taking his eyes from the road. 'You obviously couldn't find fault with the cuisine?'

'Certainly not,' she replied, staring out of her side window.

They arrived home, but before Theo could put his key in the lock Bea had opened the front door, her face ashen. 'Oh—Theo—Lily—I—I—'

They came inside quickly, shutting the door behind them, and Theo said, 'What is it, Bea?' His voice was commanding, but controlled. There was clearly something wrong.

'I cannot find Freya!' Bea practically gasped out the words, putting her hand to her mouth. 'I've searched the whole house—I haven't left the place, obviously, since you've been gone, so I know she must be here some-where, but she's just disappeared!' They could see that the older woman was shaking, and Theo immediately put a reassuring hand on her shoulder.

'Now, Bea…it's all right. We'll find her—she's prob-ably hiding somewhere…'

'Well, yes, that's what I thought. But I don't know where else to look…'

Lily squeezed Bea's arm. 'Come on,' she said calmly, 'one of us will be sure to discover where the little minx is…' But she frowned. Freya was quite a deep sleeper, and it wasn't like the child to leave her bed once she'd been tucked in.

'I've checked on all of them three times since you've been gone,' Bea said. 'About fifteen minutes ago I looked in on them again, and Freya's bed was empty. I can't understand it…'

'We'll do a systematic search, Bea,' Theo said. 'Don't worry—she can't be far.'

For the next twenty minutes the house was gone through room by room—under beds, behind cupboard doors. Although Lily wasn't really worried, a little prickle of something cold ran down her spine. This was silly. The child had to be somewhere near, safe in her own home…but where *was* she?

She looked up at Theo. 'Has Freya done this sort of thing before?' she asked, and his reply was immediate.

'Never—not to my knowledge.' He frowned, and Lily sensed that he was becoming irritated. His daughter had proved to be a difficult child to understand since his wife had gone—but she'd apparently never given them the runaround like this before.

'I wonder if she's gone outside—' Lily began, but Bea cut in.

'Oh, she wouldn't do that!' she said. 'Not at this time of night.' She hesitated. 'Although I *have* been engrossed in watching something on the box… I suppose she just might have slipped out without my knowing…'

Almost before she'd finished speaking, both Theo and Lily had reached the door together, going outside into the darkness. It had been a wonderfully warm day, and the heat still persisted as they peered around them.

Then, quietly, Lily said, 'There she is.'

Freya was curled up comfortably on the hammock, fast asleep. Theo went across straight away and looked down at his daughter, shaking his head in disbelief.

'Well, I'd have put money on her not leaving the house,' he said softly, 'but you never can tell with kids.' He was clearly relieved. They had all known that the child couldn't possibly be far away, but as each minute had passed without knowing where she was it had begun to trouble them.

By now Bea had joined them, making no bones about her relief.

'Oh, Freya,' she whispered, 'please don't ever give me a fright like that again, darling.'

Theo bent to pick Freya up, cradling her in his arms and brushing the top of her sleepy head with his lips. The child woke up with a start.

'Oh…where am I?' She yawned, looking from one to the other unconcernedly. 'Oh…I remember now…' She didn't go on, and they all went back into the house, Theo still holding her tightly.

When they got inside, he said gently, 'Now then, perhaps you'll tell us what you think you're doing outside in the garden at this time of night?' He looked down at her. 'You gave Bea a bad fright, Freya—that's not kind, is it? Were you too hot to stay in bed?'

Freya looked rueful for a moment, then turned to Lily. 'I…I went on the swing, Lily… To see if the fairy would come.'

Lily's heart gave a jolt. This was her fault! she thought.

'I was in bed for ages and ages, and I couldn't get to sleep,' Freya said. 'And then I thought if I crept downstairs I wouldn't disturb Bea, and if I went and started to swing—ever so gently, like you said—I might make the fairy come and grant me my wish…' The words tumbled out of Freya's mouth, her gaze fixed on Lily. 'But she didn't come, Lily.'

'Well, it doesn't matter now, Freya,' Theo said. 'It's high time you were back in bed.' He snuggled her into him again. 'Would you like a drink before we take you upstairs.'

'Yes, please—can I have some cold milk?'

Bea made for the kitchen. 'I'll get it,' she said at once, and Lily moved over to Freya and looked down at her fondly.

'I'm sorry if you didn't see a fairy, Freya,' she said quietly. 'But my stories are just that, sweetheart— they're stories. I make them up in my head. I told you that, didn't I?'

'Yes—but *sometimes* wishes can come true, can't they, Lily? You said that sometimes they can.'

Lily smiled. 'Yes. I believe that they can. Sometimes,' she said.

'So what were you wishing for, Freya? What were you hoping the fairy would make come true?' Theo enquired.

Freya turned her head and looked straight into his eyes. 'I was wishing what we all want...Alex and Tom-Tom and me. That Lily will never go away. That she will live with us for ever and ever and ever.'

CHAPTER NINE

THE holiday hotel was as impressive—and as welcoming—as Lily had known it would be. On their arrival they were greeted by the manager, and Theo introduced him to Lily.

'You know all of us, Barry—only too well,' he remarked. 'But this is Lily Patterson, the children's present nanny.' He glanced down at Lily. 'Barry has been looking after us for—what is it? Four years, I think—isn't it, Barry?'

The man smiled, taking in Lily's appearance. 'Yes, it must be, Mr Montague.' He paused. 'And you children are growing up so fast I hardly recognise you!' He looked down at Lily. 'I do hope you'll find your room suitable, Miss Patterson. Please let me know if there's anything else you might need.'

Lily smiled back at him. 'I'm sure it will be fine, thank you,' she murmured, thinking that although she'd spent a lot of time working in hotels, and had stayed with Sam in Rome, she'd certainly never stayed as a guest anywhere as grand as this.

Although the children wanted to rush in and inspect Lily's room, Theo was adamant that she should be given some time to herself first. 'You can all come and have a wash and tidy up,' he said firmly, pushing them in front of him into the family suite.

Alone for a few minutes, Lily went to open her window wide. Their rooms looked right over the sea, and the glorious drift of salty air filled her lungs as she breathed in deeply. Even though her emotions were so mixed up, she was determined to try and enjoy this holiday.

As she leaned pensively against the windowframe for a moment, her mind kept going back to the other evening, when Freya had slipped out of the house. Theo had not referred to it again, but Lily couldn't help feeling that the little girl's unusual behaviour had been all *her* fault. That she'd been filling the children's heads with too much make-believe. But she'd always invented stories—stories with happy endings. Which was probably something to do with the emptiness she'd felt in other ways, she mused. But was it wrong to let children think for just a little while that the impossible could happen? That wishes could come true? Surely that was what all stories were—fantasy, meant to entertain, which they had been doing for generations of children?

But she had been totally unprepared when Freya had announced what *her* wish was…that Lily could stay with them for ever. She remembered again the rush of colour that had flooded her cheeks. She hadn't looked at Theo, hadn't wanted to catch his eye or to see his expression. But he had totally ignored what Freya had said, as if he hadn't even heard it, merely taking the milk from Bea before carrying his daughter back to bed.

Now it was late afternoon, and Theo had told her that the children's supper was always served at five-thirty—obviously much later for the adults. Lily knew they must be ready for something to eat by now, so she had a quick wash, and was just brushing out her hair when an excited knocking on the door made her smile. Straight away they all burst in.

'Where are you going to sleep, Lily?' Alex asked, going across to the two single beds.

'Oh, probably the bed nearest the window,' Lily said.

'If I get fed up with the boys, can I come in and sleep in this other one sometimes?' Freya asked, sitting down and bouncing on it gently.

'If you like. Whatever Daddy says,' Lily replied. 'Come on—you must all be hungry.'

Theo was just locking their door as they all left Lily's room, and as the children scampered towards the lift he called out, 'No—let's use the stairs tonight. We all need some exercise after that long drive.'

Lily glanced up at him quickly. He'd clearly recalled her fear of lifts. 'It's quite OK, Theo—really…' she said. 'I'll be fine if I'm with all of you.'

'No, we'll go down the stairs tonight,' he repeated.

'But I wanted to work the lift!' Freya protested.

'Tomorrow,' Theo replied firmly. 'You can do it tomorrow.'

Their reserved family table was one of the large round ones near a window, and Freya plonked herself down beside Lily. 'We always sit here,' she said happily.

Soon the children were tucking into the ham-and-cheese omelettes the waitress brought, while Lily and Theo were served a pot of tea. The gentle hubbub of childish voices in the room made Lily's senses swim with pleasure at being here. Theo had described the place as child-friendly, and it was certainly that. Glancing across at him as he lounged back in his chair, she could imagine that he, too, must benefit from a time of complete relaxation in such surroundings. She watched him helping Tom butter a crust of bread, watched him lean forward to hear something Alex was saying—and wondered for the hundredth time what it must be like to have someone like him for a parent. She remembered what he'd said to her many times—that the children were the only thing that mattered in his life. He was totally engrossed in their welfare, she thought, and in the welfare of his patients. There was nothing else that mattered, or would ever matter, to him.

The days that followed had to be some of the happiest Lily had ever known. A simple routine seemed to establish itself at once. Freya would join the other slightly older children to have a tennis lesson on the hotel's courts straight after breakfast, and Lily and Theo would take the boys for a walk, or go down to the beach.

On the Thursday of the first week Lily overslept—an almost unique experience for her. Sitting up quickly, she saw that it was already eight-thirty, and, slipping off the bed, she went across to the window and out onto her tiny balcony. The hotel had its own swimming pool—which was situated almost immediately in front of their bedroom windows—to see the children were already splashing about.

They saw her standing there almost at once, and Freya called out, 'Lily, come down...we've been waiting ages for you!'

Lily waved back, and stayed to watch them for a few seconds. Theo was crouching down to encourage Tom with his strokes, then he gave a thumbs-up to Freya as she swam past him rapidly, to show off her expertise in the water… But Lily found herself drawn helplessly to the sight of Theo Montague…to his robust, athletic body. The white shorts he was wearing emphasised his strong, tanned thighs, which tensed and flexed with every movement. His dark glossy hair, shining as usual, was beginning to show the merest suggestion of greying at the temples, she noticed, but it only added to his distinguished, desirable appearance.

He knew she was watching them, and he looked up and waved briefly, his throat tightening as he saw her clad in her scanty T-shirt nightdress, her hair still in sleepy tumbles around her slender shoulders. He cursed himself inwardly for ever having introduced her into their lives. He had done it for his children's sake, yet the sight and nearness of Lily never failed to arouse him, threatening to take him off course.

He turned back to concentrate on his offspring. Soon Lily would be gone. Another line in his world would be indelibly drawn.

By the time the children were dressed for the day, and they'd all had breakfast, it was time for Freya's tennis lesson. She looked up at her father as they went outside.

'I don't want to go to my lesson today,' she said. 'I'd rather stay with you instead.'

'Sorry, Freya,' Theo said firmly. 'You said you wanted me to book you in, and it was your own idea. We just can't come and go when we like, can we? Not after we've made a promise. They'll be expecting you to turn up—they're probably waiting for you now.'

'But what if I was ill?' Freya grumbled.

'That would be different. But you're not ill, are you? So come on—no more arguments.'

Lily looked at Freya. 'Tell you what, Freya,' she said.

'I'd love to see how well you play—why don't I come and watch while Daddy takes the boys somewhere?'

That put a very different aspect on the matter. 'Brilliant!' Freya cried, then, 'Cheerio, Daddy…see you later!'

Theo smiled quickly at Lily. She seemed to know just what was needed at any given moment. 'I'll take the boys to the car museum in town,' he said. 'See you back here at eleven-thirty?'

As she turned to go with Freya, Lily spoke. 'Theo…if you would like me to stay with the children for the rest of the day I'd be only too happy,' she said tentatively. 'I mean, you've not had any time to yourself…to do what *you* want to do…and this is meant to be your holiday as well, isn't it?'

He looked at her thoughtfully for a second. 'Isn't it meant to be yours, too?' he said.

'Well…perhaps… But I am being paid to take care of your children,' she said. 'You are with them night and day, no time for yourself at all. I am their nanny, aren't I? Which should mean that you can go off and do your own thing whenever you want to…' She trailed off awkwardly. She hoped that didn't sound churlish, or as if she wanted to be rid of him!

But he smiled down at her. 'Thanks for the offer,' he said easily. 'If I get desperate you'll be the first to know.'

Later, after they'd had a light lunch on the terrace, they packed up to go down to the beach, and after a while Lily decided that she should sample the water. The children had been nagging her to join them ever since they'd arrived, but she'd felt slightly embarrassed to be undressed in front of Theo. It was true that her black tankini was not quite so revealing as her one bikini was, but it didn't leave much to the imagination. Still, she had to go along with it, so gritting her teeth and using a large beach towel, she slipped out of her underwear, cotton trousers and sun top, and was soon racing towards the water's edge, both boys holding her hands.

Theo and Freya were leading the way. Watching him as they ran ahead, Lily was struck by the slight lessening of the atmosphere between father and daughter lately. They made such an appealing sight, she thought, the dainty, long-haired little girl, with such perfect limbs and skin, and the handsome, virile man holding her hand so protectively.

The sea was so calm and warm they stayed in much longer than they'd meant to, and soon it was a mad scramble for everyone to go back and get dressed. Just as they picked their way across the shingle, Freya suddenly screamed, falling onto one knee dramatically and calling to Lily.

'Oh! Lily…look…I've hurt myself! I'm bleeding… Look! *Look!*'

Both Lily and Theo turned quickly, and were by her side in a second. Theo stooped at once to examine the damage. 'It's OK, Freya,' he said. 'It's just a little scratch from a sharp pebble, I expect.' He looked around to see if there was any glass, but there wasn't. He put an arm around her shoulder. 'Come on, get up. You'll be right as rain in a minute.'

But Freya was not going to be so easily pacified. 'Ow, *ow!*' she yelled. 'It's hurting… Lily, *you* look! See? See there?'

Now Lily stooped as well, carefully wiping some sand away from the affected area with her finger. As Theo had said, it was a small scratch, but the blood continued to trickle down Freya's big toe, and by this time Alex and Tom were also bending to have a look—both very interested in taking part in the crisis.

'Does it hurt very much, Freya?' Tom asked sympathetically.

'That's nothing, Freya,' Alex chipped in. 'Remember when I cut my finger on a piece of paper that time? Everyone said that a paper cut is *really* painful—you'll be OK.'

Lily never went anywhere without her modest first-aid kit—not since she'd been in charge of children—and she'd soon cleaned the wound and put antiseptic gel on it, before fixing a plaster in place. 'There,' she said kindly. 'Does that feel more comfy, Freya?'

Freya sniffed, not looking up at Theo, who had already changed out of his swimming trunks and was towelling the boys dry with a huge beach towel. 'A bit,' she admitted, still not wanting the occasion to pass quite so lightly. 'But it *does* hurt. Anyway, Daddy, I don't think I can put my sandals back on...not until it stops.' She paused. 'You'll have to carry me back to the hotel.'

Theo looked down at Lily, one eyebrow raised quizzically, and she glanced back at him. They both understood that Freya's dramatic injury might be a way for her to get out of her tennis commitment.

'We'll sort you out between us, Freya,' Lily said. 'But first I've brought all sorts of snacks to keep you going before suppertime. Just let me get dressed, and then you can choose from my bag.'

With Freya limping badly, they eventually made their way back to the hotel. As they entered the building, two elderly ladies gently pulled Lily to one side.

'We just *have* to tell you what a beautiful family you are,' one said quietly. 'We cannot take our eyes off you!'

'Oh—but—' Lily began, and the other woman cut in.

'As soon as we saw you come into the dining room we were enchanted. Your little girl is exactly like you, dear, and aren't the boys the living image of their daddy?'

'Well, actually…' Lily tried again. 'I really ought to explain…'

'Oh, it's natural to feel a bit embarrassed when someone like me accosts you with compliments,' one of the women said. 'But I'm not one for saying what I don't mean. And to see a delightful family like yours…so happy together…with such a pretty mother and handsome daddy. Well…'

By then the children were calling from the lift, and, making suitable pleasantries to the women, Lily escaped and rejoined them.

'What did those ladies want, Lily?' Freya asked curiously, and Lily fumbled in her handbag for a tissue to recover herself.

She'd never been good at accepting praise—not that she'd ever had much practice, and certainly not while she'd been growing up—but what had just been said to her had filled her with huge pleasure. Even if the ladies *had* got entirely the wrong idea. She liked it that she'd been thought of as an integral part of Theo's family— and more importantly that she might have been his wife…and that he might have been her lover. How strange was *that?* she thought.

'Oh—nothing,' she said vaguely. 'Something about the hairdressing facility here, that's all.' She wasn't going to tell them the truth—and she certainly wasn't going to tell Theo that they thought she was his wife! Lily knew that there was only one woman in the world who would ever have that title—and it certainly wasn't her.

Apart from the minor injury to Freya's toe, the day was deemed to have been another happy and successful one as Lily and Theo took their places in the dining room later. The children had been almost too tired to get ready for bed, so bathing had been completed in record time, and now, with the resident child-minder on duty upstairs while they enjoyed their evening meal, they, too, felt ready for a rest.

'I cannot believe the summer we're having,' Lily said, looking down at the menu. 'I think I probably got a bit sunburnt today.'

'Well, I did wonder whether you were neglecting yourself,' Theo replied, glancing across at her. 'You've been plastering the kids with protective cream ever since we arrived, but I haven't seen you putting any on your own skin.'

He studied her as he spoke, thinking how utterly ravishing she was, lightly tanned and with hardly any need for make-up—and always groomed to perfection. In spite of all she did, he'd never seen her with a broken nail or unkempt hair. He sighed inwardly and returned his attention to the menu.

After their meal they returned to their rooms, deciding to have an early night, and Theo paused outside Lily's door for a moment. 'Come in for a nightcap, Lily,' he said. 'It's only just gone ten o'clock.' He paused. 'Our balcony sports a table and chairs—and it's blissfully cool now…'

Lily hesitated. 'Won't we disturb the children?'

'No—they won't surface until morning. Not after the amount of sun and sea air they've had today,' he replied. He was looking down at her as he spoke, suddenly longing to have her to himself just for a while. Without any interruptions. Without anyone there to see them, to notice them.

'All right,' Lily said. 'As long as my nightcap can be a cup of tea.'

They let themselves into the room quietly, and Lily immediately went over to the three single beds to see the sleeping children. She half turned to Theo. 'Aren't they just…delicious, Theo?' she whispered, and he came alongside her to look down as well.

'Yes, when they're asleep,' he joked, adding, 'And most other times, too.' He paused. 'I'm so lucky to have them,' he said quietly. 'I never forget that—ever.'

Out on the balcony it was still warm. The gentle air from the sea fanned their faces, the subdued lighting in the hotel grounds adding its own magic as the water in the swimming pool shifted and glinted in the reflections.

'I shall never forget this holiday,' Lily said slowly, picking up the teapot which Theo had earlier brought to the table and filling her cup. 'It's the sort that you just wish would never end.'

Theo added a chunk of ice to his glass of whisky, swirling it around for a moment. He wanted to say that he wished so many things would never end, but now was not the time. He knew that the time would never come when he could ask Lily to forget her own ambitions and come and stay permanently. For the children she would be the perfect solution—a solution made in heaven, he thought wryly. They adored her, they trusted her, they never wanted her out of their sight… And he knew that he was beginning to feel that way, too.

He took a gulp from his glass, not looking at her, and

suddenly her closeness became too much. Without thinking, he put his glass down and leaned over to her, covering her hand with his own.

'Lily…' he began, and she looked up at him, her eyes wide, moist. 'I…I want to tell you how much… how grateful I am to you for entering our lives,' he began, not quite knowing how to go on. 'When I asked you—you know, when we were in Rome—if you would fill a temporary gap for me, just for a few months, I had no idea how indispensable you would become.'

His hand tightened on hers, and she turned her palm so that her fingers coiled into his. That simple gesture aroused him as much as if he could see her naked in front of him. But she didn't say anything. Her lips just parted, inviting…

He went on quickly. 'So…if the opportunity doesn't occur again…I just want you to know how much we've…all…loved having you in the family.' He let his hand slip away from hers and sat back, a mild exhaustion seeping through his limbs. He wanted to say so much more…but there wasn't anything else *to* say. In a few short weeks the curtain would finally come down on this part of his life. She would be gone, and they would never meet again.

She had not uttered a single word after he'd spoken, and now he looked across at her—to see that her cup was rattling in its saucer as her hands shook. He frowned and half-stood.

'Lily…are you OK? What is it? Are you ill?'

She must have caught the sun, he thought instinctively, because she was suddenly acting strangely. He took the cup and saucer from her and set it down on the table, then came around to stand beside her. Lily looked up at him, an expression on her face that he'd never seen before.

'I'm sorry,' she whispered through dry lips. 'I feel rather faint… I must lie down… I must go to my room…' She got up quickly, knocking against the table, and Theo put out his arm to steady her.

'Let me help you, Lily—I'll fetch a glass of water. Just a minute…'

'No! It's all right. I'll be all right in a minute,' she repeated. 'I just need to lie down.' She didn't stop to give even a passing glance at the sleeping children, but pulled herself away from him and made for the door. Before he could say another word she'd gone into her own room, without a backward glance.

Lily stood there, her back against the door, for maybe five, six minutes, waiting for the shaking to stop, before she slipped down to the floor and crouched, her head in her hands. She was in utter torment—worse than she'd ever experienced in her life… The touch of Theo's hand on hers had sent such a fierce passion racing through her that she had almost completely lost her senses. And it had terrified her. All the secret evils locked up in her past were coming back to taunt her.

For a few moments she allowed herself to weep silently, then she dragged herself up from the floor and went into the bathroom to get ready for bed. It had been such a perfect day, she thought, staring at her reflection in the mirror for a second, recognising the frightened, confused person looking back at her. Life should not be like this for anyone, she thought. Not for *anyone*. But she was trapped—always would be—in the fears and anxieties that pervaded her life. There was no escape. Not for her.

After an hour of tossing and turning, Lily finally lapsed into a deep sleep where dreams filtered in and out at

random. There was Theo… They were swimming together, their bodies embracing, writhing in the deep warm
water. His strong legs entwined around hers, wrapping
themselves around her, shielding her, holding her. It was
so strange, so blissful… They were in ever deeper water,
yet she could breathe without difficulty, and there was no
danger, no threat of drowning or suffocation.

They floated together effortlessly, swirling, drifting,
and as she reached up to put her arms around his neck
she could feel the tensing of his glistening muscular
shoulders beneath her touch. With one swift movement
he lifted her high above him, and she gazed down into
those black enticing eyes that were smiling at her, beckoning to her. Then he came into her bed and drew her
towards him, and their still-drenched bodies became
locked together. He was whispering to her softly…and
those gentle, sensitive hands began to slide over her, to
caress her naked limbs. His fingers were touching her,
exciting her, his mouth was on hers, their parted lips
were united in mutual seduction. His hardened body
became tense against her, and then, in slow motion, he
moved across and over her, and entered her with such
exquisite tenderness that Lily felt herself soaring with
excitement and pleasure—and relief. Relief at the impossible made possible. And in total wonderment she
heard every bird that had ever been caged singing in ex-
ultation at the ecstasy of freedom.

CHAPTER TEN

AT BREAKFAST the following morning the usual childish chatter dominated the meal around the table, but for once Lily found it hard to join in. When she had woken up she'd felt at peace with the world, but it hadn't taken her long to remember the hopeless fantasies which had filled her dreams. It had unsettled her, made her wish that her contract with the Montague family could end sooner than after the few weeks that still lay ahead.

She didn't want to look at Theo, but was even more acutely aware of his overpowering presence. Every movement he made seemed to have special significance today, she thought as she observed him, saw his strong hands reach for the jug to pour more milk into Tom's glass, lift the percolator to fill her cup with coffee.

And was it her imagination that he, too, seemed somehow different this morning? she wondered. She had seen him glance at her oddly once or twice, then look away quickly—but was that a surprise? She had left his room so suddenly last night, clearly in some sort of distress, yet had offered no explanation or excuse for it. He must be wondering what on earth was going on, but he hadn't mentioned it this morning.

And what about everything he'd said to her as they'd sat out there on the balcony…about how much he appreciated her and how perfectly she had fitted in? Praise indeed, she thought—praise for someone who received a handsome cheque each week for her trouble.

But she knew that his perceptive gaze had taken in her appearance as they'd left their rooms this morning— had felt his eyes boring into her, forming his own conclusions. And she was glad that she'd gone out of her way to look as good as usual, had showered and shampooed and perfumed, chosen a simple denim dress to wear and brushed her hair into a ponytail.

Freya touched Lily's arm briefly. 'My boiled egg wasn't as nice as the ones you do for us at home, Lily,' she said. 'The yolky bit was quite hard—yours are always dippy.'

'Well, that's because I usually only have your three to do,' Lily replied, smiling. 'The poor chef in this kitchen probably has dozens to think about—as well as all the fried ones and the poached ones…and the sausages and the bacon.'

'And they've got to cook Daddy's fish as well,' Alex chipped in. 'Daddy likes fish—don't you, Daddy?'

'I certainly do,' Theo replied. 'But I agree with Freya—Lily always manages to get it exactly right when we're at home.' He raised his eyes and held Lily's gaze for a fraction of a second. 'I would rate my breakfast today at ninety-nine per cent—while Lily's is always well past that.' He put down his knife and fork, and Lily, feeling slightly embarrassed at his words, took a slice of toast from the rack and started to butter it.

'All these compliments,' she said lightly. 'I hope I can maintain the standard when we get home…' That last word had barely left her lips when she caught her breath. She had meant to say when we get *back*. She had made the remark sound so personal, so over-familiar... It was their home, not hers. She must not allow herself such possessive thoughts and instincts. It was silly. She twisted the cap from a tiny pot of marmalade and began to spread some on her toast.

'It isn't time to go home yet, is it?' Alex asked. 'How many more sleeps have we got, Daddy?'

'Oh—about eight,' Theo replied vaguely.

He remembered Lily's words last night, when she'd said that she wished their holiday would never end, and he found himself wishing the same thing. He leaned back in his chair, folding his napkin carefully. What a situation they were in, he thought—and how on earth would the children ever accept Lily's departure? They would be heartbroken; he knew that. And there was nothing he could do about it.

One morning in the middle of the following week Lily was woken up by urgent knocking on her door, and Alex calling her name. Rubbing her eyes, she jumped out of bed and went quickly over to see what was wrong.

'It's Freya's toe!' the child exclaimed. 'It's been bleeding all over the sheets. Daddy says can you come...?'

Frowning, Lily turned to grab her white cotton housecoat from the back of the door and, shrugging it on, stopped just long enough to fetch her first-aid box before following Alex into the family suite.

Freya was sitting on the bathroom stool, holding her leg in the air as fresh blood coursed down...and crying hysterically. Theo was wringing out a flannel at the sink, and he looked up quickly as Lily came in.

'She won't let me near her. She wants you to look at it,' he said over the noise. He was bare-footed and wearing a dark green dressing gown—and was obviously still unshaven because Lily could see the dark stubble on his jaw.

She crouched down and looked up into the child's reddened face. 'Stop crying for a minute, Freya,' she said firmly. 'And let me see what's going on here.'

Almost immediately Freya's yells became more of a whimper, and with the aid of the flannel which Theo had handed her, Lily wiped firmly over the foot and examined it closely. 'I can see what's happened,' she said. She smiled reassuringly at Freya. 'While you count up to ten—you two can count as well—' she addressed the boys, who were there in the doorway like fascinated bystanders '—I shall perform one of my magic tricks.'

Bending, she took something from the first-aid kit. 'Right—start counting!' she commanded.

The three children began chanting slowly, and Lily bent her head so that Freya couldn't see what she was doing. Then carefully, deftly, with one gentle movement using a small pair of tweezers, she extracted a tiny shard of glass. She held it up triumphantly.

'Ta-da!' she said. 'You've been hiding this in your toe ever since you cut it on the beach last week, Freya—and today it was determined to escape! See?'

Theo had been standing a little way apart, and now came over to look. 'D'you think there's any more in there?' he said.

'I doubt it,' Lily said. 'This'll be a one-off. I saw the same thing happen to someone else once, and eventually these little foreign bodies do work themselves out.'

She paused. 'But we'll give this a good clean and put on a plaster.'

Now that the panic was over, Freya cheered up at once as Lily washed and dried her foot. 'It hardly hurts at all now,' she said with studied bravery. 'Not like it did before…when it really, *really* did.'

'Yes, you were a poor wounded soldier,' Lily said, 'but never mind. You're OK now, Freya.'

'I'll have to explain to Barry,' Theo said, 'about the sheets…'

'I'll do that,' Lily said. 'This sort of thing is hardly unknown in hotels.'

Theo looked down at Freya, who was leaning into Lily's side. 'If your foot is too uncomfortable to play tennis this morning, Freya,' he said, 'we can tell them when we go downstairs to breakfast.'

'Oh—no, that's OK,' Freya said airily. 'There are only two more sessions in any case. I might as well carry on.'

He smiled. 'Good for you,' he said, ruffling her hair.

Much later in the afternoon, when the children had been whisked off to watch a puppet show which had been laid on for all the youngsters in the hotel, Theo and Lily found themselves alone together by the pool. They were lying, side by side, on two sunloungers, and Theo turned his head to look at her as she relaxed, her eyes shut against the sun.

She was wearing brief navy blue shorts, which exposed her slender, tanned limbs, her small feet were thrust into white sparkly sandals, and the flimsy sun top she had on revealed her curvaceous figure just enough to excite interest… Well, it excited *his* interest, he thought honestly. He had met many women in his life, but Lily stood out as one of the most understated yet intensely desirable members of the female sex he'd ever encountered. And the funny thing was she didn't seem aware of it… She never flaunted herself in any way, either by look or gesture. He frowned slightly. He couldn't understand it—found it strange that a woman with such obvious female charms never seemed to worry one way or the other about the picture she presented to the world. She obviously took great care of her appearance at all times, no one could deny that, but it never seemed for personal publicity purposes. The way she was turned out was purely for her own benefit and satisfaction.

He turned his head away from her for a moment, wondering how she'd managed to remain single for so long. There had never been any mention of a boyfriend, and she'd been emphatic about not wanting to be tied down by marriage, or by having children of her own. And yet there was something odd about that, too, he thought. Lily Patterson wasn't only good with children, she was fantastic with them. She understood how they ticked, how to entertain them, how to deal with them— and his three had responded to her like no one else before—apart from Elspeth, of course. Even dear old Bea didn't fit in like Lily had done since she'd been with them. His three offspring seemed to consider Lily more of their own generation than as the person who was in charge of them.

She opened her eyes then, and turned to see him watching her, immediately drawing her knees up to her chin. 'I thought you were asleep,' she said softly.

He didn't answer for a moment, then, 'No—I was…' He'd been going to say, *I was watching you,* but instead said, 'I don't know what I'd have done without you this morning. Freya was determined that I was not going to have anything to do with it, or even to look at her foot. Only one person was to have that privilege—you, Lily.'

Lily shrugged. 'That's kids,' she said casually. 'If I hadn't been around she'd have *had* to let you help her.' She paused. 'Poor Freya—all that blood was quite frightening, wasn't it? But because I'd seen something like it before I guessed almost at once what the problem was.'

'Well—I was…grateful…for your assistance…' he said slowly.

Lily smiled in response, and turned her head away just as Theo's mobile rang. He reached into the pocket of his shorts to answer it. 'This is the first call I've had since we've been away,' he said, 'and I hope it isn't going to be a record-breaker. They know they can contact me from work only if it's absolutely essential,' he added, hoping fervently that their precious last few days were not going to be interrupted by any sort of crisis.

As soon as he heard the voice at the other end, his expression cleared. 'Olly!' he exclaimed. 'How're you doing?'

When Lily heard who was calling she froze for a moment. Even though the man was obviously nowhere near, the memory of his unexpected visit came back to her in a flash. Listening to Theo's one-sided conversation did nothing to give her any comfort.

'Of course you can… You know you're always welcome,' Theo said, in answer to an obvious request from Oliver. Lily turned her head away, as if to shut out the possibility that *she* might be involved in any way. 'Two weeks on Saturday, did you say?' Then, 'No, we shall be home by then.' He paused. 'I'm actually speaking to you from our holiday hotel, but we're due back on Saturday. Yes, we're having a great time…superb weather non-stop.' Another pause. 'No, really? Of course—bring her as well. It'll be good to see her again, Oliver. Now, look, you don't need to take us out to lunch on the Sunday—the amazing Lily will rustle up something for us all, I'm sure. Yes… Yes… Of course I don't mind…there's no problem. Look forward to it. Bye, Olly.' Theo snapped his phone shut and glanced across at Lily. 'That was Oliver,' he said. 'You remember he dropped by before?'

Lily nodded, her eyes closed. 'I remember,' she said briefly.

'He's asked if he and the present lady-friend can stay over—a fortnight on Saturday. There's a big party they're going to, apparently, and both our local hotels are already fully booked.' He turned away for a second. 'They don't expect to be with us until the early hours— but we'll have Sunday morning to catch up with all their news. You probably heard me say that we could offer them lunch.' He paused and glanced across at her, but Lily didn't turn her head to look at him.

'Of course I'll prepare lunch for you all,' she said simply—not bothering to add, *You're the boss, after all*.

'He's with Alice Thorpe at the moment, so he told me,' Theo went on. 'We all go back quite a long way… I wonder what she looks like now.'

Lily didn't bother to respond to that, only experiencing a sinking feeling that she was obviously going to have to be polite to Theo's boorish friend. Then she comforted herself—she'd be in bed by the time the couple returned from their party, and she'd be busy the next morning with the children, and providing lunch for

Theo's guests. She'd have no difficulty in keeping herself well occupied and out of the way. Besides, she thought reasonably, Oliver had been very drunk that last time… Surely no friend of Theo's would be an actual creep? Her over-sensitive memory had probably exaggerated the smell of the man, his overbearing closeness, she argued to herself.

After that they lapsed into the normal, easy silence that they'd both become accustomed to enjoying when they were alone together, before Theo said, 'By the way, on the last Friday evening of the season, Barry usually makes a point of providing a sort of farewell event. Dinner is served at nine—later than usual—and there's always some sort of entertainment.' He paused to wipe his sunglasses with the hem of his T-shirt and smiled across. 'We seem to be part of a pretty youngish crowd this time, who might appreciate something a bit different… Anyway, he'll warn us what to expect.'

Lily looked back at him. 'Does that mean dressing up?'

'Well, I've brought my dinner jacket just in case,' he said briefly. He paused. 'As far as you're concerned, most of what I've seen you in will do, Lily… That, um, that lemon-colour sundress would be perfect.'

Lily leaned back and closed her eyes again. She quite liked the idea of a special evening… She'd not had many of those in her life—certainly not in the company of someone like Theodore Montague—and luckily she'd packed her one and only 'occasion' number, a draped, three-quarter-length dress in shades of blue: the palest cornflower colour at the low-cut neckline, changing and floating down in varying degrees to a midnight-blue shade at the hem. It was dressy, yet casual in a summery way. Lily had taken it with her to Rome—

thinking that she and Sam might go somewhere appropriate—but if this coming Friday was to be a special one, she knew that she would feel perfectly comfortable wearing it for the first time.

Presently, the scampering of feet and energetic, childish voices announced the return of the children, and they all ran up, throwing themselves onto the sunbeds.

'Did you enjoy that?' Theo asked.

'It was great!' they chorused.

Then Freya said suddenly, obviously having waited for the right moment, 'Daddy, because of my toe and everything, can I sleep in Lily's room tonight?'

Theo looked at her sharply for a second. 'Well, I don't know,' he said. 'Aren't you happy in with the rest of us?'

'Yes…of course,' Freya said guardedly. 'It's just that—well, when we first arrived I asked Lily if I could sleep in the other bed in her room, and she said it was up to you.' She hesitated. 'I was thinking just now that— what if my toe starts bleeding again in the night? You'd have to call Lily, and disturb everyone, but if I was there with her in the first place it might save everyone a lot of trouble.'

Theo smiled his crooked smile. 'If Lily doesn't mind—' he began.

'Of course I don't mind,' Lily said. She smiled at Freya. 'It'll be just us girls—and I hope you don't snore!'

As they were leaving the dining room later on—after the children had eaten their supper—Barry met them in the hall.

'Hello again, everyone,' he said jovially. 'My goodness—what weather you brought with you! You're all beginning to look like polished conkers!' He turned to Theo.

'Supper will be late on Friday night,' he said. 'It'll be served at nine, and I've booked a local band—they're excellent—to entertain us for a few hours afterwards.'

'Sounds wonderful,' Theo said, glancing at Lily. He realised that he knew very little about her likes and dislikes, what branch of the arts, or of the musical world in general, that she preferred. He bit his lip. It didn't matter one way or the other what she liked, he thought. Soon it would be nothing to do with him.

'I'm going to sleep in Lily's room tonight,' Freya told the manager. 'Because of my toe.'

'Yes—I heard about your poor toe,' Barry said sympathetically. 'Is it OK now, Freya?'

'Well—it *nearly* is… But I'm sleeping in with Lily just to make sure.'

The man grinned. Lily had spoken to him about the soiled sheets, and he'd assured her that that kind of thing was all in a day's work for his staff. 'Well, don't go stepping on glass again, will you?' he said. 'You're much too beautiful to go spoiling your looks—even if it was only your toe that was damaged.'

It wasn't long until bedtime, and the children seemed extra tired tonight, Lily thought. Tom had almost fallen asleep over his warm milk at the table, and even Alex seemed quiet.

'I think we should do some colouring or play a game now,' she said lightly. 'We've all had enough exercise for today. I could show you some card tricks, or—'

'Yes! Let's play cards!' Alex said. 'I know a trick, Lily. I'll show you…'

Lily looked up at Theo quickly, realising how natural it had become for her to make decisions for the family. She hadn't bothered to see what Theo wanted them to do. Over the long holiday it had become the norm for them to automatically share the responsibility. She had not once been made to feel like the employed nanny, or as if she should check with him as to what his opinion was. They seemed to have slipped unconsciously into the smooth running of everything they did with neither of them querying the other.

She had to admit that the routine seemed to suit Theo well enough. He was relaxed, unhurried, and appeared to be totally content. And the almost uninterrupted sunshine had served him well—his handsome face was devoid of the occasional brooding appearance she'd been aware of once or twice at home, and the frown line across the broad forehead was almost invisible. It had obviously been time for him to have a complete rest from his work and to recharge his batteries.

When it was time for bed Lily went into the family suite, as usual, to get them all bathed, with Theo agreeing to sit out on the balcony and let her do it alone.

'I don't think this is going to take long.' She smiled. 'Everyone seems exhausted tonight.'

Later, after they had had their own meal, and had spent some time in the lounge with a drink, Lily excused herself.

'I think I'll go up,' she said, getting up from her chair and looking down at Theo. 'I feel as tired as the children today.'

He half stood, his whisky glass in his hand. 'Yes— go and have a good rest, Lily.' He paused. 'I hope my daughter doesn't keep you awake—on any pretext. She can be a little madam at times…and seems to have acquired a talent for twisting people around her little finger. Don't let her take advantage of you.'

Lily shook her head quickly at the suggestion. 'Goodnight, then.'

'Goodnight, Lily.'

He watched her go, conscious of the glances of other men in the room. She must be used to turning heads, he thought, yet she seemed totally unaware of it.

Lily let herself quietly into her bedroom. Freya was curled up on the other single bed, her long fair hair tumbling over the pillow, and Lily moved across to look down at her. Soon this whole episode, her time with the Montagues, would be a distant memory, and the thought brought a terrible lump to her throat. She wished that she'd never met Theo on that journey to Rome. All he had done was disrupt her life, cause her to question her own feelings, her own ambitions, and remind her that the sort of life she was enjoying—no, *revelling* in—would never be hers in her own right. The happiness she was experiencing was second-hand, lent to her for a fleeting few weeks. And then it would be back to normal…to treading her way cautiously, to protecting herself, protecting her emotions. To living her life outside the accepted parameters of other human beings.

Suddenly Freya leapt up and flung her arms around Lily's neck. 'Boo!' she cried. 'I haven't been asleep… I've been waiting for you!'

Lily stepped back in surprise. 'You little monkey! I thought you were fast asleep.' She uncoiled herself from the child's hold and stepped back, sitting on the side of the bed for a moment. 'It's late, Freya—you're going to be very tired in the morning…'

Freya sat up, hugging her knees and looking at Lily

with her large, sensitive eyes. 'I hate Daddy,' she said. 'I was waiting up to tell you that. I hate him.'

The statement was matter-of-fact, and came as an unpleasant surprise to Lily. But her face remained expressionless, and she let a few moments elapse before replying—equally matter-of-factly. 'I hate my mother,' she said coolly.

Now it was Freya's turn to be caught unawares. 'You…hate your *mother*, Lily?' she said. 'Why…? Why on earth would you hate your mother?' The thought was preposterous to Freya. 'No one hates their mother… do they?'

'I do,' Lily said, still sitting where she was, sensing that there was much more to come in this conversation.

'But—*why?* What…what did she do?' Lily's revelation was much more interesting to Freya than her own statement had been.

'Because she gave me away,' Lily said simply—and even after all this time tears sprang to her eyes. 'She didn't want me, Freya, so she gave me away to someone else.'

Freya sat forward and hugged Lily to her desperately. 'Oh, Lily…why would your mother do that?' She paused, gulping. 'My mother would never, never have given *me* away!'

Lily shrugged. 'I don't know, really,' she said slowly. 'I think she was very young. And—and she wasn't married to my father. Perhaps she didn't have any money of her own to buy me food and look after me.'

Freya pulled away slightly and gazed up into Lily's face. 'I don't know why anyone would want to give *you* away, Lily,' she said slowly. 'You're lovely. We all love you—and Daddy loves you, too.' She paused. 'Do you like Daddy, Lily?'

'I do like him,' Lily replied carefully, then, 'But why do you hate Daddy, Freya? You did say that, didn't you?'

Freya's expression changed in an instant. 'Because he let Mummy die,' she said flatly.

The bald statement took Lily's breath away, and she had to wait a moment before going on. 'What do you mean?'

Freya shrugged. 'Well, he's a doctor, isn't he? Doctors make people better—they don't let them die.'

'Freya—don't you think that Daddy *wanted* your mother to get better? Don't you think that he tried every way he knew to make her better?'

Freya shrugged. 'Well, he didn't try hard enough, did he? And anyway—' she paused '—he's not sad. Not like Alex and Tom-Tom and me are.'

Lily felt helplessness sweep over her. This was difficult ground that she was being asked to cover. She realised that the little girl—with all her common sense and grown-up ways—was confused and unhappy. No wonder there had been tension between her and her father if the children really thought Theo could have saved his wife if he'd tried harder. It beggared belief. Yet how understandable it would be to their innocent minds. Doctors were there to make people better.

She leaned over and took Freya in her arms, holding her close. 'How do you know that Daddy isn't sad?' she asked softly.

'Because he never cries,' Freya said at once. 'We've never, never seen him cry. Not once. Not even on the day Mummy died. He just stood there looking cross, with a funny look on his face. Everyone cries if they're sad, don't they?'

Lily hugged her even closer. 'Freya, listen to me,' she said, trying to keep the urgency from her tone. 'I can promise you, with my hand on my heart, that Daddy would have done everything in the whole wide world to make Mummy better… But even doctors—even the very best of them—can't always succeed. That's just the way it is.' She rocked Freya gently for a moment. 'I know that Daddy loved Mummy very, very much. I can tell when I see him looking at her photograph some-times. And…' She paused. 'And I'm also sure that Daddy does cry sometimes, when he's by himself. Not when he's with you…because he doesn't want you all to be made even sadder. Would… Would you have felt any happier if you *had* seen him cry?'

'No-ooo…' Freya said slowly. 'I don't *want* to see Daddy cry… I just thought it strange that he never did, that's all. But I don't want him to cry.' She paused. 'We wish that he could make you stay, Lily… But he's told us that it wouldn't be fair because you've got lots of other things you want to do.' She looked into Lily's eyes again. 'He said he didn't think you particularly wanted to work with children…that you were going travelling and stuff…but I said that if he tried really hard he could *make* you stay.'

Lily lifted back the duvet and laid Freya down gently. 'Let's not talk about that now, Freya,' she said. 'You really must get to sleep. But…' She paused. 'But maybe I could stay on for a bit longer—we'll see, shall we?' She dropped a kiss on Freya's forehead. 'One thing I must make you promise me, Freya—never, never say that you hate Daddy. Because he loves you all so much—all he wants is for you to be together, nice and cosy, even without Mummy. So—promise?'

Freya snuggled down. 'I promise—and *you* must promise not to say you hate your mummy, either, Lily…'

Lily smiled. 'Yes, I promise not to say that ever again,' she said truthfully. Because who could ever know just what it had cost her mother to part with her two small babies? Her life must have been full of contradictions and problems—things that, still only in her teens, she had been unable to deal with. 'So—we don't hate anyone, do we, Freya?' she said.

Freya was getting drowsy, a slight smile on her cherubic lips. 'No. We don't hate anyone, Lily,' she said. 'Not our daddies and mummies, anyway.'

CHAPTER ELEVEN

As Lily stepped into her dress on the final Friday evening of their holiday, she found it hard to believe that they had only been away for two weeks. To her, it seemed so much longer than that… She and Theo and the children had covered so much ground, being together for practically the whole time, with each day providing yet more insight into their lives. It had been a wonderful time for all of them, with only two damp mornings to contend with. And apart from a few minor quarrels between the children, not to mention the toe incident, there had been nothing to spoil what had been, for Lily, the best two weeks of her life.

She sighed briefly, staring at herself in the mirror for a second and meeting her own frank gaze. A dreadful feeling of finality swept over her. Time was running out for her, and much worse was knowing that soon the children were going to have to get used to another person looking after them. Although she'd said to Freya during their very revealing talk the other night that she might stay on for a while, Lily knew that it would only prolong the agony if she did. It was time, she thought, to move on—to find the elusive 'something' that would give her fulfilment, help her to reach the goal in life that she hadn't yet put a name to.

Thanks to her lightly suntanned skin, there was hardly any need for her to wear much make-up, but she did brush a little colour on to her cheeks and lips, patting her hair into place for a final time. She'd decided at the last minute not to leave it loose, but to wind it up into a knot on top, letting one or two wavy strands escape around her face. Then, last of all, she massaged some of her precious perfume into her neck and behind her ears.

It was already gone nine when Theo tapped lightly on her door, and when she opened it her mouth dried. He seemed even taller tonight, as he stood there in the dimly lit corridor, his shoulders broader in the expensive, immaculate evening suit he was wearing, his hair dark and glossy, enhancing the strong forehead, the penetrating, searching eyes as he looked down at her.

In one brief moment he took in her appearance, too. To him, she resembled a dainty fairy princess…she only needed a tinselled wand in her hand! He cleared his throat.

'That's a very nice dress, Lily,' he said rather formally, as she locked her door.

'Is it OK…? Will it do?' she asked innocently.

He smiled briefly. 'It will do very well,' he said.

As they went towards the lift they met the nanny who kept constant watch on their floor when parents were absent, and she smiled across at them as they passed.

'Have a good evening,' she said pleasantly.

'You won't hear a thing from our three,' Theo said easily. 'I almost had to wake them up to get them ready for bed.'

As they entered the dining room Lily's breath was almost taken away. It had been transformed, with small tables now surrounding a space in the centre from where the carpet had been rolled away. And practically the only lighting in the room was provided by numerous flickering candles.

'Goodness—doesn't it look…beautiful?' Lily said, as they stood for a moment waiting to be seated.

In another time in his life Theo might have replied, *As beautiful as you.* Instead, he said, 'Barry has a very shrewd idea of the theatrical—this is supposed to be a treat for busy parents, perhaps to take them back to earlier, more romantic times.' He paused. 'Barry likes this to be a memorable last evening for everyone.'

A waiter appeared then, and they were shown to a table just a little way behind the ones nearest the centre of the room. Almost at once the band began taking up position, briefly tuning their instruments, and Lily looked across at Theo.

'I suppose people dance?' she asked, nodding towards the polished oak floor.

'Some do,' he said casually. 'If they want to.'

Lily picked up the menu which the waiter had just given her, feeling relieved. There was obviously no obligation to join the dancers, she thought, which was just as well because she didn't have a clue. She'd never danced with anyone in her life. But she wondered about Theo. She looked at him quickly over the top of her menu. He would be very stylish, elegant—and was no doubt competent in any arena. She imagined him gliding effortlessly around the dance floor, with Elspeth held protectively in his arms.

Lily's eyes misted for a second. They'd have been the most glamorous couple in the room, she thought. How he must miss her. Especially on this particular evening. Instead of his wife being here he had to put up with the children's nanny instead, and, stupidly, Lily wished she could, just for a short while, magic herself into someone else.

But if Theo was feeling nostalgic he certainly didn't show it as he looked across at her over the candlelight, his eyes glistening. 'Have you chosen what you'd like, Lily?' he asked, forcing her gaze to remain locked in his. He paused. 'You know, I'm ashamed to admit it, but it'll be something of a pleasure not to have to make up my own mind every evening next week. It'll be good to be presented with whatever you've cooked for us— knowing that I'll enjoy every bit of it.'

Lily coloured up at his words, and returned her attention to the menu. 'Thanks for that,' she said lightly. 'And I'm happy to say that I shan't mind being back in harness again.' She paused. 'This has been a great holiday, Theo… Thank you so, so much for inviting me to come as well.' She didn't say, *and for footing the bill, paying for every single thing*—because that would have spoilt it.

He didn't answer immediately, but looked at her with such an expression in his eyes that Lily's colour would have deepened even further if she'd noticed it. There was so much he wanted to say—so much he *could* say— but there were no words, and again, for the second time in his life, Theodore Montague felt helpless. Then he shrugged, a slight frown creasing his forehead, his masculinity taking over. This situation *would* be dealt with—*he* would deal with it. Experience was a good teacher, and it had shown him before that every problem became solved eventually, one way or another. It would be no different this time.

'By the way, I must say again that I was impressed

at how you sorted Freya and her toe out,' he said casually. 'Have you had nursing experience, Lily—or first aid?'

Lily smiled at that. 'No—'fraid not. I suppose my reaction to the situation came out of long experience of having to look out for myself—to keep on my toes and not to get fazed under pressure, that's all.'

That was something of an exaggeration, she thought, because she often *did* get fazed. The trick was in not letting it show.

Once the band were ready, the music started playing at just the right level of sound, making sure that the diners could communicate without having to shout at each other, and once again the menu was varied, the food perfectly cooked.

'That pheasant was superb,' Lily said appreciatively as she put down her knife and fork. 'It can be a tricky beast to get right, but the chef has managed to pull it off—as usual.'

Theo nodded. 'I shouldn't think that Barry has many complaints,' he said.

Lily shook her head. 'You'd be surprised. You can bend over backwards to please everyone, and sometimes there are still those who nit-pick. I've known one or two in my time,' she added. 'But it's an occupational hazard we were taught to accept.'

As soon as the main course had been eaten, one or two couples began to take to the floor. The music was simple, rhythmically, and, studying them as they moved, Lily observed that there didn't seem to be any particular pattern to the steps. It seemed more or less a question of moving from one foot to the other, keeping time with the music. If she was really forced to, she thought, she could probably join in with that without falling over or making a fool of herself.

Suddenly Theo leaned forward, his elbows on the table, and Lily turned her attention away from the dancers for a moment.

'Tonight I feel as though all my birthdays have come at once, Lily,' he murmured, and Lily's heart jumped in her chest. He was clearly going to say something important, she knew that at once, but what was it? And could she deal with it?

'Oh?' she said uncertainly. 'Why?'

He waited for a moment before going on. Then, 'Because I've got my little daughter back at last,' he said simply. 'And it's completely blown me away.' He reached for his glass of wine. 'I'd got them all into their pyjamas tonight—Tom was actually already asleep, and Alex was cleaning his teeth in the bathroom—and I was sitting out on the balcony for a moment.' He paused. 'Freya came up to me and climbed onto my lap. She put her arms around my neck…and told me that she loved me.' He drank quickly from his glass. 'She has not got that close to me, nor uttered those words, since Elspeth died. I…I…feel as if a huge shadow has been moved away, letting in the light again.'

Lily found it hard to speak for a moment. So Freya had taken everything she'd said the other night to heart, and had begun to understand her father. Involuntarily Lily reached out and touched Theo's hand, and he immediately responded, curling her fingers in his.

'It was only a matter of time, Theo,' she said gently. 'Children, especially little girls, feel things more deeply than anyone realises. Of course she loves you. She's never stopped loving you.'

'I was getting a bit worried,' he confessed, not letting Lily's hand go. 'And—to make it even better—she's asked to give up on boarding at school. She wants to come home each night, as she used to do. Which pleases me more than I can say. Now we'll be complete again… Well, not quite…' he added quickly. 'But you know what I mean.'

Lily felt a huge wave of emotion well up inside her. It was almost too good to be true, she thought, but the expression on Theo's face said it all. Freya had come back to him.

Just then their waiter brought the dessert menu, and they were both glad to concentrate on that for a moment—to distance themselves from the briefly charged atmosphere. After they'd placed their order, Theo leaned forward again.

'I have to say, Lily, that I feel your hand in this—in Freya's turnaround—' he began, but she cut in.

'Oh, I doubt it, Theo. Don't forget we've all had a super holiday. Everyone's relaxed and…'

'No, it's more than that,' he said. 'That couldn't account for it. I've made sure that the children have had good times, plenty of diversions since they've been without their mother. But it's only since you've been with us that I've seen a distinct change in Freya. And tonight my daughter confirmed what I've been hoping for for so long.'

Listening to his words, Lily felt that all *her* birthdays had come at once, too. It was so touching to see Theo's relief—and if she had been responsible for somehow bringing that about then she could only be glad. Theo was a good man—a loving, caring, generous father, who deserved to be loved totally in return. It must have been agonising for him to feel rejected by the daughter he clearly worshipped.

'Well,' she said brightly, determined not to let any residual sadness cloud the evening, 'that puts the icing on the cake, doesn't it? We won't ask for another thing!'

Suddenly, slowly, he got to his feet and came over to stand beside her. She looked up at him, her eyebrows raised slightly.

'May I have the pleasure of this dance, Lily?' he said, and she answered quickly.

'I don't know how to… I've never danced with any-one before…' she began.

The thought of a man holding her close had always filled her with dread, but Theo took her by the arm gently, raising her to her feet.

'There's really nothing to it, Lily,' he said quietly. 'I'll show you.'

He led her onto the floor—which was by now crowded, with practically everyone in the room joining in.

'Just let your body move with mine, with the rhythm,' he said softly.

And Lily found that it was a lot easier than she could ever have imagined, with Theo's strong arm around her waist, his hand holding hers firmly. Amazingly, her dreaded horror of feeling a masculine form melding with hers had evaporated, and what she was feeling at that moment was not only acceptable, but terrifyingly attractive and desirable. And as he eased her more closely to him, so that she could feel the warmth of his body penetrate the fine fabric of her dress, Lily felt an exciting tremor ripple through her, making her momen-tarily literally weak at the knees.

The dance, such as it was, demanded nothing more

than to keep time with the beat, and as they swayed together, neither speaking, Lily smiled faintly to herself. This was her very first experience of being with a man in this situation, and she knew that it would never happen again. This was a one-off, and for these precious few minutes Lily felt herself transported to some un-dreamed-of world—a world far away from anything to do with *her*.

When the music stopped no one moved back to their tables. Almost at once it began again, and the dancing continued. Lily could just feel the touch of Theo's chin resting on the top of her head as they swayed together, and the slight, intimate sensation she felt set her emotions rocketing again, sent the blood coursing through her veins at breakneck speed.

After a while they returned to their table, just as the waiter was bringing their coffee, and Theo leaned towards Lily again.

'Of course,' he said, his tone serious, 'there's another very plausible explanation for my daughter's change of heart.'

'Oh?' Lily stirred sugar into her coffee, glancing up at him.

'Yes, I wonder—have been wondering—could it possibly be Jasmine weaving her magic again?'

Lily was nearly caught off guard at that. Oh, no! she thought. How embarrassing! Those fairy stories of hers were not meant for adult ears! She clicked her tongue. 'What have the children been telling you?' she said.

'Well, I've had all the stories you've told faithfully recounted,' he said, 'and I know that when your Eve starts to play on the swing in her garden a fairy called Jasmine suddenly appears and they have long talks. Tell each other everything. And I know that Jasmine makes wishes come true…makes frightened people brave… makes horrid people become nice people.'

Lily covered her mouth with her hand. 'Oh, honestly, Theo… I'm sorry if the children have been wasting your time telling you all that stuff…all that nonsense…'

'It's not nonsense, Lily,' he said. 'Your stories took them to a land of make-believe, made them feel happy and contented before going to sleep, made them think that wonderful things can sometimes happen.' He paused. 'My problem is that I was expected to go on with it—to make up some myself. I told them that those particular stories belong to you, and that you are the only one who knows what the endings are.' He smiled. 'I'm relieved to say that they understood that and stopped pestering me.'

Lily shook her head briefly. 'I'm sorry—I'm afraid it's a legacy from my own childhood,' she said. 'I used to get myself to sleep at night by pretending that there were knights in shining armour to rescue me, or animals who could lead me out of danger in a dark wood…stuff like that.' She made a face. 'And I take full responsibility for Freya letting herself out into the garden that night,' she went on seriously. 'That *had* to be my fault.'

He shrugged. 'She was perfectly safe,' he said. 'The only harm done was to poor Bea, who got a bit worried. But it was short-lived.'

He held her gaze for a moment, and that slow, slightly crooked smile played around the elegant mouth. 'Actually,' he said, 'I'd very much appreciate it if you would tell *me* a story, Lily… You know, one with a happy ending.' He leaned towards her again. 'D'you think that if I wished really hard Jasmine would wave her magic wand in *my* direction?'

CHAPTER TWELVE

'WHEN are you going to be cooking all this food, Lily?'
Freya asked, as the three children helped her to lift the
supermarket bags into the boot of the car.

'Oh—I'll be preparing most of it tomorrow, I expect,'
Lily said, 'and the rest on Sunday morning.'

'Are we going to have some of it, too?' Alex asked.
'Or is it just for Daddy's friends?'

'Of course you'll have some, too!' Lily exclaimed.
'We'll have ours in the kitchen—but you can help me lay
the table in the dining room for Daddy and his guests.'

They had been back from their holiday for almost
two weeks, and the next day Oliver and his girlfriend
were due to visit. Although Lily was not looking forward to seeing the man again, she was determined that
the meal she presented for their Sunday lunch would be
special. In fact, she was looking forward to thinking it
out and preparing it. For Theo's sake.

Since their return life had very quickly returned to
normal, with Theo absorbed in his work and Lily automatically reverting to employee mode. Even though life was
good, with the children quite content to be back home, the
easy familiarity of those sun-filled days between her and

Theo had sort of eroded. It was as if a switch had been thrown, bringing them back down to earth.

She had thought so much about their time away, and Lily was honest enough to admit that one of the high points had been that last Friday evening. As she and Theo had danced together she'd felt so blissfully content, so cherished, so protected—she'd wished they could have stayed there like that for ever. It had been an incredible sensation which she had never expected would ever enter her life. And she'd been conscious that when they'd returned to their table he had been as briefly subdued as she was—as if something precious had been theirs for those few moments, only to slip away, like quicksilver, just out of reach.

Theo had been so busy since their return—not only leaving early most days for the hospital, but also spending hours in his study preparing lectures. Some evenings he came down so late for his supper that by the time he did Lily had already had hers. But she realised that he was having to clear the huge backlog which had piled up while they'd been away. So when he eventually did appear, looking thoughtful and preoccupied, she would put his meal in front of him, wish him goodnight, then go and leave him in peace.

That evening, as she went past him, he put out a hand and caught her arm briefly. 'Are you avoiding me, Lily?' he asked, half-jokingly. 'As I come in, you go out.'

She glanced up at him quickly. 'Of course I'm not avoiding you,' she said. 'I… I just thought you needed time for yourself, that's all. Without having to engage in pointless chit-chat.'

'What we usually talk about is seldom pointless,' he

said. 'Stay and talk—unless you've other things you have to do?'

Lily turned immediately to do as she was told, making herself a cup of tea before sitting opposite him as he began his meal.

'I've hardly had a chance to see anything of the kids,' he said ruefully, reaching for his glass of wine and looking across at her. 'Have they been behaving themselves?'

Lily smiled, helping herself to one of the shortbread biscuits she'd made and arranged on a dish for him to have with his coffee later. 'Your children are never any trouble,' she said firmly. She noticed that he was eating rather slowly, and she said hesitantly, 'Is everything all right, Theo? The meat hasn't dried, has it?' Well, it wouldn't be her fault if it had, she thought. It had been waiting to be eaten for some time.

'No, of course it isn't dry—it's good, as usual.' He paused. 'I was just thinking that we really must get this nanny thing sorted soon… It's sort of…not exactly slipped my mind…but gone on the back burner lately, shall we say?'

Lily sighed inwardly, hesitating before responding to his remark. Then, 'Look, Theo—you've clearly got enough to be thinking about at the moment,' she said. 'If necessary I can delay my departure—at least for another month, if that'll help. Don't worry about the children for now…we'll get it sorted all in good time.'

His expression cleared straight away. 'Well, that would take the heat out of the situation if you could—would—stay on for a bit longer,' he said. He stopped eating and looked straight into her eyes. 'Thank you,' he said simply.

Neither of them spoke for a few moments, then Lily

said, 'I've been thinking about lunch on Sunday, Theo—' she began, but he interrupted.

'Oh, there's no need for you to beat yourself up about that, Lily,' he said. 'Olly and Alice are known for their healthy appetites—I know that whatever you put in front of them will be hoovered up in five minutes flat.'

Lily shrugged. 'Well, anyway, I thought I'd give them asparagus mousse to start, followed by steak and stilton royale with baked tomatoes. It presents very well, and is really delicious.'

'I'm sure it is,' Theo replied, somewhat dryly.

'I usually serve it with new potatoes and fresh green vegetables,' she said.

He looked across at her as she spoke. She obviously really enjoyed cooking, and she was so good at it—good at everything, including looking after other people's children—which she'd said she did *not* enjoy. He glanced at her as she sipped at her mug of tea. If only she could see her way to staying with them permanently he wouldn't have a care in the world. But how could he expect that of her? She was young. She had her own life to live in the way *she* wanted—not to please others.

'And then I thought I'd do a favourite of mine for dessert,' Lily went on, leaning her elbow on the table and cupping her chin in her hand. '*Gâteau Meringue de la Forêt Noire*—it's full of cherries and almonds and fresh cream. It's an indulgence, I admit, but you haven't asked me to do any special entertaining since I've been here, so I'd be happy to push the boat out. And to keep my hand in at the same time.' She paused. 'You never know, I might have to return to the cookery world one day. If my dream of finding that special something I'm looking for never comes true.'

* * *

It was very late on Saturday night when Theo's friends came back from their function. Lily, who'd gone to bed early but hadn't yet managed to sleep a wink, heard Theo greet them. Glancing at her bedroom clock, she saw that it was gone one. Even though her room was on the second floor, she could clearly make out Oliver's rather rough voice—so unlike Theo's cultured tones, she thought instinctively—and a woman's strident giggle. They were all obviously chatting in the hallway. There was a sudden burst of laughter, then she heard the sitting room door being closed firmly, and the sounds became inaudible.

They were probably going to spend half the night going over old times, Lily thought, turning over and giving her pillow a thump. She frowned slightly. The room set aside for them was on the first floor, almost next to the boys. She hoped they'd come up quietly and not disturb them…

The next morning Lily was up early, as usual. She went into the bathroom and ran a brush through her hair, staring at herself in the mirror. Was it her imagination, or was she looking a bit tired this morning? she asked herself. She shrugged. How she looked was of no importance—her presence would be swallowed up by that of Theo's friends, she knew that for sure. She hadn't yet made Alice's acquaintance, but if Oliver was any indication Lily knew exactly what the woman would be like. Just hearing her giggle and her high-pitched voice had been enough.

In spite of those preconceptions, Lily decided to make the best of herself, even though she wouldn't be with the adults much… Her flimsy cotton floral skirt teamed with a low-neck cream blouse would be light and unrestricting. She knew that the outfit suited her in an understated way, and worn with flat, strappy sandals it gave a slightly peasant-like effect. Perfect to wear on a warm Sunday morning, busy in the kitchen, she thought. And although leaving her hair loose would have looked good, Lily decided to tie it back in a ponytail as she was cooking.

She switched on the shower, biting her lip for a second. She wondered whether Oliver remembered the rather embarrassing incident between them the last time they had met. He had been very drunk at the time, she mused, and probably hadn't given the matter another thought... She wished she could say the same. She could still feel the man's presence overcrowding her.

She could hear that the children were awake, so she went down to the boys' room. Freya was there, too, and they all leapt up to hug Lily as she went in.

'Have Daddy's friends arrived?' Alex asked.

'They have,' Lily replied. 'So don't make too much noise, because they're probably still fast asleep.'

'I'm telling the boys one of your stories,' Freya said importantly. 'I've nearly finished it.'

'Good for you,' Lily said. 'And don't forget it must have a happy ending!'

After they'd got ready for the day, the children went on down to the kitchen. Just as Lily was about to follow them, she bumped into Theo at the top of the stairs.

'Good morning, Lily,' he said quietly, taking in her appearance at a glance.

'Morning, Theo,' she said lightly, going past him and running down the stairs. 'I expect you're ready for some coffee?'

'Oh, I've had mine,' he replied, coming down and following her into the kitchen, where the children were doing some colouring. He went over and kissed the top of each of their heads. 'I hope we didn't disturb you last night?' he said. 'There was a bit of noise, I'm afraid.' He glanced at Lily, who was busying herself getting the breakfasts. 'I shouldn't bother with anything for Olly and Alice,' he added. 'They won't surface until midday.'

She glanced up at him. 'Oh? Well, that's OK, then. We'll concentrate on lunch instead.'

'Yes—we're helping Lily to lay the table and everything,' Freya said.

'Don't overdo it,' Theo murmured affectionately.

After breakfast he went out into the garden with the children, leaving Lily in peace. She felt perfectly relaxed about her lunch party—she'd cooked this particular menu many times before, and it had always been well received. She found herself humming a little tune as she lifted the ingredients from the fridge and switched on the oven. She really did enjoy cooking for people, she thought. It gave her great satisfaction to present good, appetising food attractively.

Suddenly a voice right behind her made her start, and she turned to see a woman standing there. 'Oh—hello— you're… You must be Alice?' she said pleasantly.

The woman's black hair, hanging in untidy curls down to her shoulders, framed a rather hard face, and she was clad in a bright green shiny housecoat. She gave a barely perceptible smile as she went across to the sink. 'Yes, I'm Alice,' she said, 'and I'm badly in need of a glass of water to take a couple of tablets.' She put her hand to her forehead. 'We did have rather a good time at the do last night. I have no idea when Oliver will see the light of day. He's virtually unconscious at the moment.'

Lily took a tumbler down from the cabinet and filled

it with water, handing it to the woman, who made a grimace as she swallowed the pills.

'Ugh—the smell of cooking is getting to me in here,' Alice said. 'Sorry—but I'll have to leave... Where's Theo? Is he up?'

'Yes, he's outside with the children,' Lily said shortly, turning back to what she was doing.

Alice came to stand beside her for a moment, looking her up and down, taking note of what she was wearing. 'Theo was telling us what a wonderful find you are,' she drawled. 'He hasn't had much luck with staff before, apparently, and suddenly you appear out of the blue. Not only good with his kids, but a great cook to boot. Well, well... Very convenient for him.' She paused. 'But do be warned...Lily. It is Lily, isn't it? In case you've been wondering, Theo is not on the market. Nor ever will be, I'm afraid. It's a sad loss to the female race in general, but there you go. I wouldn't want you to have any false hopes.' She smiled a superior smile. 'I expect you have an eye for the main chance—but don't get your hopes up, will you?'

Lily was angry at the woman's words, and turned to stare at her, her face hot. 'I take offence at your remarks,' she said, her voice steely. 'I am an employee here. I am not looking for anything more. I have no plans—at least not the sort you've just alluded to.'

'Well, that's all right, then,' Alice said smoothly. 'We go back a very long way, you know... Theo and I were...close at one time...and I know the guy. Shop's shut, I'm afraid.'

She left the kitchen then, and Lily stood rooted to the spot, shaking inside at what had just been said. How could *anyone* think that she had designs on Theo, or that she was looking for a relationship? That a complete stranger should make that assumption was insulting—and degrading. If only they knew—if only any of them knew—just what her feelings were in that direction!

For a few moments she felt unable to carry on with doing the meal, then she pulled herself together. Why was she letting the wretched woman get to her like this? Alice whatever-her-name-was was a complete nobody, and her unlooked-for comments and advice were of no interest whatsoever.

Almost at once Lily calmed down and got on with the job in hand. She heard someone coming down the stairs—it could only be Oliver, she thought—and then heard him go through into the garden. Just so long as he didn't come in here, bothering her, she thought.

After a few moments Theo came in and stood watching her for a second or two.

'I'm going to make some coffee for them,' he said briefly. 'They don't want anything to eat, apparently. Anyway, I told them to save their appetites for lunch.'

'Fine,' Lily said coolly. 'Will one-thirty be about right?'

'Perfect,' he replied, wishing with all his heart that it was just going to be the five of them, as usual. He was already tiring of his friends' company.

Just then the children came in as well, and Lily said, 'Yes, it's about time we laid the table. Freya—fetch the napkins from that drawer, please.'

Lily had to admit how attractive it all looked by the time they'd finished. The expensive glassware and cutlery on the snowy white cloth looked like something from an advertisement.

When it was nearly time to serve the meal Lily sent the children upstairs to wash, just as Theo came into the dining room to fetch some drinks to take out into the garden. He glanced down at the table, frowning.

'Why only three places?' he asked.

Lily shrugged. 'Because there are only three of you,' she replied.

'And what about you?' he demanded—almost curtly. 'Why aren't you eating with us?'

'Because I always have my lunch with the children,' she pointed out patiently, not bothering to add that the thought of having to sit and talk to Theo's guests filled her with distaste.

'Then in that case the children will eat with us as well,' he said, in a tone of voice which brooked no argument. In a sudden, unusual gesture he caught Lily's wrist firmly. 'You are not a kitchen maid, Lily,' he said. 'Please don't act like one.'

The determined expression on his face made Lily catch her breath for a moment, but she merely nodded. 'OK—fine,' she said. 'The children will enjoy being with everyone, I'm sure.'

She was right. They were thrilled to be invited to be part of the occasion, and they all behaved impeccably—which was no surprise to Lily. Even little Tom was made to feel important by not having to wear his bib but being given a napkin like everyone else.

Although the meal had turned out perfectly, with Theo and Oliver doing it great justice by clearing their plates, Alice merely toyed with her food, leaving most of it untouched. She looked over at Lily.

'So sorry not to be able to eat much of this,' she said, 'but I'm afraid I have no appetite today… We ate—and drank—too well last night.'

'Don't worry about it, Alice. The rest of us will make up for it,' Theo said easily, glancing over at Lily and winking at her briefly. 'That was absolutely fantastic, Lily—you're a genius.' He smiled at the children. 'Not a crumb left on the plates over on that side of the table,' he observed.

'It was deeeeelicious!' Alex said, scraping around his dessert bowl. 'Can I have some more, Lily?'

'I think you've had enough for now, Alex,' she said. 'But you can have some more for supper.'

Oliver lounged back in his chair, lacing his fingers across his ample stomach and staring at Lily, who was sitting immediately opposite him.

'Are there any more where you come from, Lily?' he asked lazily. 'I think you're the sort of woman we should all have in our homes.'

Lily looked back at him quickly. She had been conscious of him staring at her now and again during the meal, with a strange look in his eyes, and she wondered if he *did* remember how she'd almost thrown him away from her that night. She shivered involuntarily, hating the sight of his thick, podgy fingers as he held his wine glass, hating the florid face and double chin.

'I can tell you now, Olly, that people like Lily are not to be found—she is a rare treasure. So hands off!' Theo said.

'I wouldn't say no to a bit of hands-on,' Oliver said crudely, and at once Theo got up from the table.

'Come on—I found that book I was telling you about. It's in the sitting room.'

After a few minutes Alice took herself back to bed—she hadn't even bothered to get dressed—while Oliver went into the television room to watch the motor racing. Before joining him, Theo put his head around the kitchen door.

'Thank you again for that super meal,' he said. 'And by the way, they're staying over tonight as well... Alice is apparently not well enough to go home.' He made a face as he said it, but Lily ignored that—they were his guests, and they could stay as long as he wanted them to. But she groaned inwardly. She didn't feel comfortable with either of them—especially after the things Alice had said to her earlier.

'I've promised to take the children to the park this afternoon,' she said. 'So we'll be out of your hair.' She paused. 'There are two freshly made cakes in the pantry if they need something with their tea.'

Theo held up his hand. 'I shouldn't think any of us need much more food for the rest of the day,' he said. 'I'll look after them now, Lily. You've done more than your fair share.'

Thankfully, Lily didn't see much of Theo's guests after that. Oliver spent the afternoon snoring in front of the television, while Theo apparently went to his study to work. And it wasn't until much later that Alice emerged to join the men in the sitting room.

To Lily, it had seemed one of the longest days of her life. Although Alice had said she wasn't well enough to eat lunch, Lily felt that the woman had been deliberately picky—pushing the food around her plate, and leaning back in her chair and staring at the children. Even though everyone else had enjoyed it, her attitude had put a noticeable damper on the occasion. Thinking about it, Lily couldn't imagine that Alice had ever meant anything special to Theo, whatever she'd said. She knew him well enough to know that the woman wasn't his type. But then, did she *really* know? she asked herself. She knew nothing of Theo's past—as he certainly didn't know anything of hers.

It was almost midnight when Lily, only half-awake, thought she heard Tom whimpering in the room below. She had been so tired at bedtime that she'd fallen into the deepest sleep she could ever remember—a sleep full of words and faces, of anxieties about the future, about the children, and about Theo. And in amongst all that there was Alice, sneering at her, and Oliver, who kept on touching her face and neck, but she couldn't tell Theo about it because they were friends and it would upset him.

At last, she managed to drag herself into a sitting position, and, yawning, pushed her hair away from her face, listening again for the sound which had woken her. It was quiet now, but just to make sure Lily slid out of bed. Not even bothering to put on her dressing gown, she padded in her bare feet down the stairs to the boys' room. She pushed open the door gently and looked down at them, at their sleeping, peaceful faces. There was nothing wrong, she thought. She must have imagined it. Or dreamed it.

Turning, she crept out of the room—and was confronted by Oliver, who stood there dressed only in a pair of boxer shorts, his hairless chest gleaming slightly with perspiration.

'Oh…' Lily gasped, overcome with embarrassment at being there wearing just her short T-shirt nightie. She recoiled at his large figure barring her way. 'I hope I haven't disturbed you,' she said, moving away quickly. 'I thought one of the children was awake, that's all.'

She could smell the overpowering odour of whisky on his breath, making her teeth chatter slightly in alarm. The familiar edginess crowded in on her, making her eyes huge with fright as she tried to go back up the stairs to her room.

'Don't go—don't run away,' he said, his voice thick. 'I like you, Lily. I liked you before, didn't I? Only you didn't seem to like me.' He paused, grinning down at her. 'We could have some fun.' He moved towards her slowly. 'You're not shy, are you, Lily? Pretty woman like you must have had quite a few experiences…'

He leered down at her, and Lily was so terrified that she couldn't even swallow, her throat was so dry. He had made it impossible for her to get back to her own room, and she glanced desperately towards Theo's door. She'd go in there and wake him if she had to. Anything to get out of this situation.

Following her gaze, Oliver smiled slowly. 'Theo was called out on an emergency at the hospital,' he said, 'just as we were all going to bed. Said he'd be back by the morning.' He cupped her chin in his hand. 'I like you, Lily,' he said again, stupidly.

Lily's heart was thumping so loudly now that she thought it would choke her. She pushed at his chest with her fists. 'Get away from me,' she breathed. 'How dare you behave like this? You're a guest in this house— get out of my *way*.'

She was shaking so violently that she thought she was going to faint. She knew she had to do something now, before he went any further and there was no time. No time. Quick—quick, go *now*… Without thinking, she turned and ran quickly down the stairs, thrusting open the front door and running away—running, running, her emotions wildly out of control, tears pouring down her cheeks. But she was free, she was out of his orbit, she could escape…

As she pelted blindly along, Lily wasn't even aware of the pavement's rough surface under her feet. The street was completely deserted, and there was no traffic… There was nothing and no one to witness her terrified flight. But after a minute or two the cool night air on her flaming face began to calm her down, and her steps became a slower walking pace. Then, abruptly, she stopped by a lamppost, putting her arms around it and hugging it for support, resting her forehead against its cold surface, waiting and waiting for the passing of time to restore her senses.

Then she stood stock still, the realisation of what she had just done hitting her like a brick. She had left the children alone…left them alone with that man in the house… In her own frenzied panic she had abandoned them! How *could* she have done that?

After a moment, realising that she could actually stand unaided, she let her arms slide down, away from the lamppost—just as Theo drove alongside her. He pulled up sharply with a screech of brakes and got out—and without a word he wrapped his body around hers, almost lifting her off her feet. For several moments he just stared down into her tear-soaked face.

'For God's sake, Lily…what's going on?' he said.

And Lily clung to him, letting the feel of him through her scanty nightwear warm and console her. 'I'm so sorry,' she whispered. 'I'm sorry…'

He said no more, just half-lifted her into the car, then

drove rapidly the few hundred yards home. Lily sat with her head back against the seat, her eyes closed.

They reached the house. The front door was still open, as she'd left it, and there was no sound. Without a word Theo ran up the stairs two at a time, to check on the children. Then he came back down more slowly, and with his arm around Lily's waist led her gently into the kitchen, closing the door behind them. He put his arms around her again tightly, tucking her head under his chin, and began rocking her gently. And as Lily's heart-rate began to slowly return to normal the tears began to flow freely.

Once the worst was over he led her to one of the arm-chairs and sat her down, then knelt on the floor beside her, looking up at her. Her hair tumbled untidily around her face, which was pale and wet with tears, and her eyes were huge. Every now and then a discernible tremor rippled through her slight body. He took a hand-kerchief from his pocket and wiped her cheeks tenderly.

'Talk to me, Lily,' he said gently. 'Talk to me, please.'

Lily knew that if she started unburdening herself to Theodore Montague her tears would begin again—but she knew that she had to do it. Surely he deserved an explanation for tonight's behaviour? But could he ever understand?

He tried to help her. 'What frightened you, Lily?' he asked. 'What were you running away from?'

Lily took a deep breath, her innate common sense and self-control taking over at last. 'It was all my fault—' she began. Well, what else could she say? Oliver hadn't actually done anything—he'd barely touched her. All he had done was revive the past that she'd spent so much of her life trying to forget, to push away from her. And he'd done it so well! For those few awful moments she'd been a helpless child again, subject to adult expectations, demands and desires. And she'd been trapped—as she'd been so many times before. 'I went down to the boys' room because I thought one of them was awake,' she began.

'And someone else was there as well?' he offered.

She hesitated. 'Oliver was standing there, and…' She couldn't explain.

Theo's expression was grim. 'What did he do, Lily? Did he try it on?'

Theo's perceptiveness made it easy, and now Lily's words came quickly.

'Well…sort of…' she said. 'But…what he's proved to me again is that I still can't cope. I will never be able to cope…' She looked down anxiously into Theo's eyes.

'Cope with what?'

'With life. With myself,' Lily said simply. 'I'm lost, Theo. I'm only half a person. I'm useless.'

He couldn't stand seeing her distress any longer, and he pulled her to her feet, enfolding her in his arms again, letting the silence wash around them for a few moments.

'Will you marry me, Lily?' he whispered. 'I want you…so badly.'

His unbelievable declaration, made in this unbelievable situation, made Lily draw back in amazement—and dismay. He didn't know her—not really. Emotionally she was a complete stranger.

'Why would you want a wife like me?' she asked him hopelessly. 'You don't know me, Theo, and I know nothing—*nothing*—of love. I only know lust. I'm damaged goods. Not a sound investment for any thinking man. I'm not a whole person. I'm only half a person. Who wants to settle for fifty per cent of anything?'

'Go on,' he said quietly.

And for the first time in her life Lily was able to unburden herself to a man—to a man she could trust utterly.

'Sam and I never knew our parents,' she said slowly. 'We were given up as babies by our mother—a single parent. Sam was fostered—happily, I believe—while I...' She swallowed, choking back the dark years. 'I went from one home to another. In one particular place I was forced to fend off the unwanted attentions of a man who was supposed to be protecting me...a man who seemed so kind at first, but who wanted more... more.' Lily shivered, her teeth chattering uncontrollably for a moment, and Theo's hold on her increased gently, his expression becoming even grimmer as he began to get the picture.

'Didn't you tell anyone?' he said softly. 'Wasn't there anyone to help you?'

'I tried a couple of times,' Lily said. 'But no one believed me—or they preferred not to believe me. In the end I didn't really believe myself. I gave up trying to explain—stopped trusting any man who came near me. I just ran away all the time. I was soon categorised as an impossible, difficult child that no one wanted to know. But even when I went into a children's home it didn't stop. Every man I came across I saw as a potential danger... even though most of them were not. I lost all my grip on reality. My only obsession was staying...pure.' That last whispered word was almost inaudible.

Theo's voice was gruff. 'I can't bear to think of it,' he said. 'I can't bear to believe it.'

'I know,' Lily said. 'And that was the prevailing attitude. There was no one I could turn to.' She looked up into his face. 'So you see, Theo…I know I would be useless as a wife—because I would be afraid to have feelings, to love you. I am afraid of myself.' She paused. 'I wouldn't know how to please you…'

Theo held her even closer to him. 'Well,' he said, 'you're doing all right at the moment, Lily.' He smiled gently. 'We all have to start somewhere—and I can wait for you. There's no rush. And I'll show you the way, if you'll give me the chance.'

Then, as she continued looking up at him, his mouth closed softly over her parted lips. And Lily didn't pull away—didn't want to pull away, letting his masculinity overpower her, take her over completely, in the first awakenings of a new life, thrilling her mind, body and soul. She was alive at last—alive to love and to be loved.

And his obvious physical need for her as she felt the hardening of his body against her vulnerable frame didn't repel or disgust her. It only made her want to know him fully, as her lover.

Neither of them wanted to move, or to break the spell which bound them at that moment, then he whispered in her ear, 'You have become everything to me, Lily. I don't know what I've done to deserve this second chance—if you'll have me—but I know I could make you happy. I just know that we could be happy together.' Then he paused. 'But I'm forgetting something, aren't I? Forgetting that you have other plans—that you're looking for another answer in your life.'

She put a finger over his lips gently. 'I think I've already found it,' she said. 'I think it's been here all the time.' She closed her eyes, praying with all her heart that she wasn't going to suddenly wake up.

'So…do I have to go down on one knee, Lily Patterson? To beg you to be mine?' he said.

She nestled into him, loving the strong, handsome face, the searching gaze, the seductive mouth.

'No need for that, Theodore Montague,' she said dreamily. 'I'm yours already. Now and for ever.'

Bestselling Harlequin Presents author

Lynne Graham

brings you an exciting new miniseries:

PREGNANT BRIDES

Inexperienced and expecting, they're forced to marry

Collect them all:

DESERT PRINCE, BRIDE OF INNOCENCE

January 2010

RUTHLESS MAGNATE, CONVENIENT WIFE

February 2010

GREEK TYCOON, INEXPERIENCED MISTRESS

March 2010

www.eHarlequin.com

HPI2884

TWO CROWNS, TWO ISLANDS, ONE LEGACY

A royal family torn apart by pride and its lust for power, reunited by purity and passion

Harlequin Presents is proud to bring you the final two installments from The Royal House of Karedes. As the stories unfold, secrets and sins from the past are revealed and desire, love and passion war with royal duty!

Look for:

RUTHLESS BOSS, ROYAL MISTRESS
by Natalie Anderson
January 2010

THE DESERT KING'S HOUSEKEEPER BRIDE
by Carol Marinelli
February 2010

www.eHarlequin.com

HP12883

HARLEQUIN *Presents* EXTRA

Presents Extra brings you
two new exciting collections!

MISTRESS BRIDES
*When temporary arrangements
become permanent!*

The Millionaire's Rebellious Mistress #85
by CATHERINE GEORGE

Da Silva's Mistress #86
by TINA DUNCAN

MEDITERRANEAN TYCOONS
At the ruthless tycoon's mercy

Kyriakis's Innocent Mistress #87
by DIANA HAMILTON

The Mediterranean's Wife by Contract #88
by KATHRYN ROSS

Available January 2010

www.eHarlequin.com

HPE0110R

REQUEST YOUR FREE BOOKS!

HARLEQUIN *Presents* ®

PASSION GUARANTEED SEDUCTION

2 FREE NOVELS PLUS 2 FREE GIFTS!

YES! Please send me 2 FREE Harlequin Presents® novels and my 2 FREE gifts (gifts are worth about $10). After receiving them, if I don't wish to receive any more books, I can return the shipping statement marked "cancel". If I don't cancel, I will receive 6 brand-new novels every month and be billed just $4.05 per book in the U.S. or $4.74 per book in Canada. That's a savings of close to 15% off the cover price! It's quite a bargain! Shipping and handling is just 50¢ per book*. I understand that accepting the 2 free books and gifts places me under no obligation to buy anything. I can always return a shipment and cancel at any time. Even if I never buy another book, the two free books and gifts are mine to keep forever.

106 HDN EYRQ 306 HDN EYR2

Name _____ (PLEASE PRINT) _____

Address _____ Apt. # _____

City _____ State/Prov. _____ Zip/Postal Code _____

Signature (if under 18, a parent or guardian must sign)

Mail to the **Harlequin Reader Service:**
IN U.S.A.: P.O. Box 1867, Buffalo, NY 14240-1867
IN CANADA: P.O. Box 609, Fort Erie, Ontario L2A 5X3

Not valid to current subscribers of Harlequin Presents books.

Are you a current subscriber of Harlequin Presents books and want to receive the larger-print edition? Call 1-800-873-8635 today!

* Terms and prices subject to change without notice. Prices do not include applicable taxes. Sales tax applicable in N.Y. Canadian residents will be charged applicable provincial taxes and GST. Offer not valid in Quebec. This offer is limited to one order per household. All orders subject to approval. Credit or debit balances in a customer's account(s) may be offset by any other outstanding balance owed by or to the customer. Please allow 4 to 6 weeks for delivery. Offer available while quantities last.

Your Privacy: Harlequin Books is committed to protecting your privacy. Our Privacy Policy is available online at www.eHarlequin.com or upon request from the Reader Service. From time to time we make our lists of customers available to reputable third parties who may have a product or service of interest to you. If you would prefer we not share your name and address, please check here. ☐

HP09R

HARLEQUIN *Presents*

AT HIS *Service*

From glass slippers to silk sheets

Once upon a time there was a humble housekeeper.
Proud but poor, she went to work for a charming and
ruthless rich man!

She thought her place was below stairs—
but her gorgeous boss had other ideas.

Her place was in the bedroom, between his
luxurious silk sheets.

Stripped of her threadbare uniform, buxom and blushing
in his bed, she'll discover that a woman's work has never
been so much fun!

Look out for:

POWERFUL ITALIAN, PENNILESS HOUSEKEEPER

by India Grey

#2886

Available January 2010

www.eHarlequin.com

HP12886

Stay up-to-date on all your romance-reading news with the brand-new Harlequin *Inside Romance!*

The Harlequin *Inside Romance* is a **FREE** quarterly newsletter highlighting our upcoming series releases and promotions!

Click on the *Inside Romance* link on the front page of www.eHarlequin.com or e-mail us at InsideRomance@Harlequin.ca to sign up to receive your FREE newsletter today!

You can also subscribe by writing to us at: HARLEQUIN BOOKS
Attention: Customer Service Department
P.O. Box 9057, Buffalo, NY 14269-9057

Please allow 4-6 weeks for delivery of the first issue by mail.

IRNBPAQ309

HARLEQUIN
Ambassadors

Want to share your passion for reading Harlequin® Books?

Become a Harlequin Ambassador!

Harlequin Ambassadors are a group of passionate and well-connected readers who are willing to share their joy of reading Harlequin® books with family and friends.

You'll be sent all the tools you need to spark great conversation, including free books!

All we ask is that you share the romance with your friends and family!

You'll also be invited to have a say in new book ideas and exchange opinions with women just like you!

To see if you qualify* to be a Harlequin Ambassador, please visit **www.HarlequinAmbassadors.com.**

*Please note that not everyone who applies to be a Harlequin Ambassador will qualify. For more information please visit www.HarlequinAmbassadors.com.

Thank you for your participation.

BAP09BPA

I ♥

HARLEQUIN® *Presents*

BROUGHT TO YOU BY FANS OF
HARLEQUIN PRESENTS.

We are its editors and authors
and biggest fans—and we'd
love to hear from YOU!

Subscribe today to our online blog at
www.iheartpresents.com

HPBLOG